the

GREATEST LOVER

of

Last Tuesday

the

GREATEST LOVER

of

Last Tuesday

NEIL McKINNON

*To Dot.
All the Best
Neil McK___
2015*

thistledown press

Thistledown Press Ltd.
410 2nd Avenue North
Saskatoon, Saskatchewan, S7K 2C3
www.thistledownpress.com

Library and Archives Canada Cataloguing in Publication

McKinnon, Neil, 1941–, author
The greatest lover of last Tuesday / Neil McKinnon.

Issued in print and electronic formats.
ISBN 978-1-77187-062-7 (pbk.).–ISBN 978-1-77187-072-6 (html).–
ISBN 978-1-77187-073-3 (pdf)
I. Title.

PS8625.K556G74 2015   C813'.6   C2015-900488-8
C2015-900489-6

Cover and book design by Jackie Forrie
Printed and bound in Canada

This book is a work of fiction. Names, characters, places and incidents are either products of the author's imagination or are used fictitiously. Any resemblance to actual events, locales or persons, living or dead, is entirely coincidental.

Thistledown Press gratefully acknowledges the financial assistance of the Canada Council for the Arts, the Saskatchewan Arts Board, and the Government of Canada through the Canada Book Fund for its publishing program.

the

GREATEST LOVER

of

Last Tuesday

For Ren and Callum

CONTENTS

Author's Note

I FIRST MET ALBERTO CAMELO IN THE city of Xalapa in the Mexican State of Veracruz where I had gone to be alone as my marriage was suffering its first frost. We struck up a conversation in a restaurant and I warmed to him immediately. He took an understated pleasure in his own existence — a pleasure which I found to be an enticing antidote to the cynicism that surrounds much of everyday life. He was then in his nineties and his long-time companion, Adriana had died a few years before.

Alberto was not a resident of Xalapa, nor was he Mexican although he now lived in Guadalajara. He was on his way to the port city of Veracruz which he tried to visit as often as possible because, in his view, it was the most romantic city in the world and he retained fond memories of many pleasurable entanglements that had their genesis in the city's music-filled evenings.

He took an interest in the plight of my marriage, offering his story in the hope that I would find a remedy for the malaise that was currently smothering my happiness. I found his tales compelling and suggested publication. He agreed on the condition that it not happen until he had left this world to go to what he called, "a less than inspiring place." We kept in touch and because I visited Mexico frequently we were able to meet a number of times.

Alberto had started to record his life when he was eighty and I have made use of his many notebooks in recreating the most salient episodes. As he aged it became difficult for him to write and I began taping our conversations for later transcription.

He confessed that for a time after Adriana's death he had considered dying himself. However, death was not an option as he was addicted to life, his health was good, and he had no violent enemies. So he determined to accelerate his remaining time in this world by finding joy one day at a time. He said that those who deny their age with trite phrases such as, "you are only as old as you feel," are simply fools who rebuff reality in order to delude themselves. The key is to embrace the journey to old age and like any other journey, to enjoy the diversions and detours along the way. "The trip itself is exciting," he said, "while the destination is no doubt vastly overrated."

The story that you are about to read is as faithful a reproduction of Alberto's and Adriana's lives as I can make it. I have taken liberties in only two ways: (1) In accordance with Alberto's wishes, I have altered the text where it was necessary to hide identities, and (2) Alberto recounted his stories as they occurred to him. I have attempted to put everything down in the correct chronology. Near the end, he was little help in this respect as his memory sometimes confused the order of things. One exception is the opening chapter, located first at Alberto's request. He felt it important that the reader be aware, from the outset, of some of his personal difficulties. However, though the order may be imperfect, extensive checking has tended to confirm the details of events exactly as he recalled them.

Neil McKinnon
Lake Chapala, Mexico
November 13, 2014

Drinks with Dinner

THE SETTING WAS TRANQUIL BUT ADRIANA was in a bad mood. We were drinking our morning coffee on the second floor balcony at Don Emilio's. The mountains on the far shore of Lake Albatross created a murky backdrop for blue water, and treetops between us and the lake made a green carpet broken only by occasional white cupolas and patches of purple jacaranda.

Twice that morning we had been disturbed by individuals who were collecting signatures that they needed to force others to alter their behaviour. "They make me angry," she said. "I detest those who want to impose their morality on everyone else. It's offensive. Why don't you write about that?"

"You're out of touch as usual, my titillating tyro of turpitude. I have written about it."

"Tell me," she demanded.

"Certainly, but keep your interruptions to a minimum."

"You can trust me," she said.

"Very well. It occurred to me, that while my primary intent is to expound on the various permutations and combinations of love, and on the types of individuals who search for, find, and participate in that commodity, I should also be completely honest about some of the roadblocks that I've encountered on my own path to romance."

"What roadblocks?"

"I'm thinking about personal imperfections."

"Writing about *your* faults could take forever."

"Not so. I don't propose to discuss all of my transgressions. Rather, my exposition will deal only with those behaviours that are intrinsic to my character and which some have labelled as indecent, immoral, or decadent. These characteristics have contributed considerably to my life's enjoyment. There is much to be said for decadence, although, at times, it restricted my progress toward my main goal — perfecting the art of love."

Her eyes widened. "You're pulling my foot."

"No, I'm not. Our society not only raises obstacles to the enjoyment of love, it tries to keep us from the pleasures of profligacy. We're surrounded by plagues of militant prudes and fitness extremists who are hell-bent on constructing an antiseptic world that exhibits about as much charm as flatulence in a crowded room. The objective of these insipid rule-makers is to enact enough restrictions so that they and others of their ilk will never be vexed, whereas being vexed is a major part of life."

She smiled. "Now you're scratching my elbow. Do you expect others to constantly aggravate you?"

"Yes I do and I expect to aggravate others. For instance, I'm not fond of garlic breath, women who volunteer their medical history, children who whine, men with a perm and anyone who allows a dog to defecate where I plan to step. God's sense of irony constantly puts me in the path of these people."

"I understand. Given your personality, that train runs in two directions."

"Of course it does. Scripturally, it could be said that, thou offends me and methinks I, thee."

"I see. So what is the point . . . to be perpetually offensive and offended?"

"No, to use a cliché, it is to live and let live. The rule-makers think that the whole purpose of existence is to gossip, petition and engage in lawsuits . . . and they are winning. Their targets are now little more than trees condemned to stand uncomplaining as they are urinated on by the puritanical dogs of self-improvement."

"But things don't stay the same. How do we ever keep up with the changing nature of what behaviour is correct and what is incorrect?"

"We can't; it is useless to try to keep pace with current moral imperatives. Everything we yearn for today will eventually become verboten. Reprobates are always the first to be deleted when evolution deals with human desires — think of tobacco. Without new transgressors the world might be uncomplicated and sanitary, but it would also be bland, colourless and unappetizing."

"I agree with everything you say, though you sound like those you preach against. Enlighten me further, my dissolute do-gooder. What sins do you recommend?"

I thought for a moment. "Much has been written about the various modes of unacceptable pleasure. I will, however, confine my discourse to those that are known as temptations of the flesh. The most fashionable and enjoyable of these are intemperance and lust."

"Very well," Adriana said. "Tell me your perversions. Have you ever descended from your moral mountain long enough to experience that of which you speak?"

"Of course, like all who are young, I experimented with different forms of depravity."

"Name one . . . and spitting on the street doesn't count."

"If I must. One of the activities most frowned upon is over indulgence in strong drink."

"I have already detected that you are not unfamiliar with Uncle Brandy. Did you have more than a passing acquaintance with some of his relatives?"

"Yes, I did . . . a very close relationship — so close that one particular episode caused me to examine my life and vow to control my intake — a vow that I failed to keep. There was a time when my mind did not properly supervise my behaviour."

Adriana ordered a refill for her coffee. "This I must hear," she said.

"What I'm about to say is appropriate for two reasons. First, it illustrates how a character flaw came near to derailing my search for true love, and second, part of it happened in this very establishment."

❧

One day I arose at three o'clock in the afternoon nursing a terrible hangover that I had acquired at a formal dinner party thrown by our mayor, Carlos Windsock, to honour the new Bishop of Aguas Profundas, a dinner to which I was invited because of my late father's friendship with the mayor. I had wakened earlier but each time I tried to get up, the ceiling descended and pinned me to the bed. My head felt like a terminal disease and my teeth had torn ligaments. The room looked as if an army had conducted war games, but I had no memory of the events of the previous evening. I hung my skull over the sink and poured pots of cold water over it to comfort my temples. Then I dressed and made my way to Don Emilio's to try and eat, walking with small steps so as to not jar my throbbing cranium.

As I entered the restaurant I spotted Eloisa Garza, a woman who, by the time she was twenty, had already spoken all of the words that the Lord had allotted for her lifetime. Her voice is easily mistaken for the bray of a sick burro. She has a personality that curdles milk and her face resembles homemade soap. Long ago, Eloisa had decided that only she could save me from my own imperfections.

I retreated immediately but she saw me and called my name. I do not believe that I was yet driving sober mental transportation or I would have kept walking. Instead, I went to her table. She was seated alone. "Yes, Eloisa, what do you want?"

"Hello Alberto. You don't look so good. Are you okay?"

She's perceptive, I thought. *She senses my previous night's debauchery.* Out loud I asked, "Do I look that bad?"

"You're acceptable. We should have a drink."

"God no, I couldn't look at a drink."

"You didn't say that last night."

"Don't tell me you were at the dinner. Did I behave?"

"Of course you did. Can't you remember?"

"That's a relief. No, I don't recall anything."

"You don't remember the bishop?"

"What about the bishop?"

"Well, there was a small incident."

"What kind of an incident?"

"Just minor. The bishop was a little displeased when you recited poetry while he was trying to give thanks for the meal."

"That must have been delightful. What poetry?"

"It was a poem about a lady with tattoos."

"I recited 'The Tattooed Lady' during the blessing! My God, everyone must hate me."

"Well not quite during the blessing. You started another poem . . . about a girl from Nantucket. To get you to stop, the bishop asked you to say grace."

"Me! I don't know any prayers. What did I say?"

"I don't remember your exact words . . . you proposed a toast to the Holy Ghost. Then you knocked back three for the Trinity."

My stomach limped toward my throat and the room swung to starboard. I reached for a chair and sat down. "I'm going to be sick. What else happened?"

"There was another very tiny incident during the meal."

"More bad news . . . what was it?"

"It was nothing really. The Bishop had been talking about the miracle of the loaves and the fishes. You announced that anybody could turn water into wine, but only *you* could perform a real miracle — turn a chicken into a fruit. Then you put a drumstick in your pocket, walked over to the governor's mother and told her that if she felt in your pants she would find a real peach."

"Is that when they threw me out? Surely they didn't let me stay."

"No, some suggested it but the mayor talked them out of it. Later, the mayor himself got a little miffed but the bishop calmed him down."

"Oh no, what else did I do?"

"You didn't do anything. His wife should have handled it herself."

"Please say I didn't do anything lewd."

"No, you didn't. She found you funny . . . until the cigarette."

"Cigarette? Did I burn her?"

"No, she was never in any real danger."

"Tell me . . . what happened?"

"You insisted that she have a cigarette even though she doesn't smoke. You used a candle from the table to light it and somehow the table cloth caught fire. It flared quickly because of the brandy you had spilled."

"What next? Did I put out the fire?"

"Not exactly. A lady screamed and two men ran to get water but they hesitated when you commanded everyone to stay seated. Then you stood on your chair and prayed for wet weather. The room remained dry so you descended from the chair and did a rain dance. The tablecloth was still burning so you also took some precautionary action."

"What kind of precautionary action?"

"You kept the mayor's wife from catching on fire."

"You mean I did something right."

"You certainly did and they should thank you. You created a firewall by pouring red wine over her."

"Thank God she didn't get burned. She was okay, wasn't she?"

"Well, not exactly. A spark landed on her dress and started to smoulder. You tried to rip away the burning part but unfortunately the whole dress came off."

"Oh no, they threw me out then, right?"

"No they didn't. Everyone seemed in a trance, but you took charge. You said that a gentleman shouldn't allow a lady to be half-naked in public. Then you took off your pants and gave them to her."

"Oh God, what next?"

"I don't know. That's when I took you to another room to find you some trousers."

"Then what, did I get sick?"

"I took you home. You were so sweet, telling me that I'm the only one, revealing the crush you had on me in school and saying it wasn't necessary to wait until we got married. It was my first time and I'll always treasure it. It was also my second, third and fourth time — the most marvellous night of my life".

"It . . . it . . . it . . . was?"

"We're so fortunate," she said. "We'll raise a wonderful family. I can hardly wait to tell the whole world . . . but first we'll have to do something about your drinking."

❦

Adriana chortled into her cup. "You haven't told me about that part of your life," she said. "Did you stop drinking? Did you and Eloisa get married? What happened?"

"I became Eloisa's project. She made it her goal to turn me into a teetotaller."

"A project, what did she do?"

"Ultimately she had marriage in mind, but I never intended to trade my freedom for sobriety. I knew that the path to alcoholic bliss was the same trail that led away from Eloisa's grasp. To paraphrase Socrates, at that age I firmly believed that, an un-sodden life was not worth living."

"How did Eloisa deal with that reality?"

"She read my intentions and decided that a slow approach was best. Accordingly, she developed a step-by-step program to which she gave the acronym SET, Special Events Tapering. It was predicated on the idea that knowledge is power, that if I was aware of the situations where I drank too much then I would be forearmed should I encounter similar events in the future. She supplied me with a notebook and every time I took a drink I was to write down the circumstances surrounding that drink. For example, if I encountered my old school chum Gilberto on my way to the post office and we happened to be near a bar and stopped in, then presumably by referencing my notes, I would know enough to take a different route the next time I had to mail a letter.

"The system worked reasonably well in the beginning. Then I found that I could make it more efficient by writing down the event before actually having a drink. Soon I had a master list to which I could refer whenever I felt thirsty. For example, I could simply look at my list, write myself a letter and walk by Gilberto's house on the way to mail it. As well, I was able to list contingency items: wedding toasts for all my single friends and drinks to mitigate the sadness I would feel when each of them should die. My list continued to expand and soon, on a recurring basis, I was toasting my marriage, the birth of my first child, my divorce and my ex-wife's funeral. Eventually, I regularly imbibed to celebrate my own passing. At that point, Eloisa decided that the system wasn't working."

The waiter brought fresh coffee. "I imagine that was the end of it," Adriana said. "Surely Eloisa gave up."

"No she didn't. Her middle name is Stubborn. She decided that I needed the discipline of a formal plan. She developed a system she called DDT, Different Drinks Tapering, where drinking was permissible but only at important celebrations. Before starting DDT, Eloisa had me rank all drinks in order of my preference. I began the list with my favourite brandy and progressed down through tequila, rum and scotch, eventually arriving at my least favourite, gin.Whenever I was allowed to drink, I was to start with my favourite and work my way down the list. The theory was that one will under imbibe if every new drink is worse than the last one.

"DDT had two flaws. First, the definition of important celebration was not rigid, so a double brandy became a prelude to tying my shoes and a single shot was required every time I went to the bathroom. Second, I found that if I made my first brandy large enough, I could entertain the illusion that all subsequent drinks were of equal quality. I became skilled at deceiving my taste buds into believing that the worst home grown gin was really Cognac."

Adriana toyed with her cup. "I think you needed a reward system — perhaps a chart like those in elementary school where you are given a gold star for good behaviour. Eloisa could have called it Alberto's Stopping Schedule. At least it would have had an appropriate acronym."

"She was way ahead of you, old Big And Talking. She had a large jar and every time that I had a success, she put a coloured bead into it. She intended to set the date for our wedding when the jar was full, an incentive that had little attraction for me."

"What happened? Were you unable to fill the jar?"

"Exactly! After six months it contained only three beads. My performance was so lacking that I never had to remove beads from the jar. About then Eloisa gave up."

"What did she do?"

"She abandoned me for a non-drinking singing evangelist from the United States."

Adriana pursed her lips. "You must have altered your life. You would be dead if you had continued with that behaviour."

"Exact again, that is one reason that I'm penning my memoir. Apart from explicating love, it will remind me of my imperfections, one of which is a great love for Uncle Brandy and all his relatives. I also hope to show how I was able to become a great lover despite a number of errors that the Good Lord made in my design."

The morning had been long and I had drunk too much coffee. I excused myself to go to the toilet. When I returned, I found that Adriana had paid the bill. We walked in silence — she to her home and I to mine next door — while I ruminated on what I remembered of those early days. Perhaps Eloisa's systems had failed because no imposed blueprint, program, timetable or list can repair another's behaviour. I alone, am qualified to fix myself.

Feasting on Passion Mountain

NOW THAT YOU, THE READER, HAVE been forewarned that mine is a character not without defects, and now that I have achieved the dubious status of octogenarian, I, Alberto Camelo, have decided to continue unloading my memory in order to let the world know how it was that I overcame my flaws to become the greatest lover of this or any other century.

I did not take this decision lightly knowing full well that there are many who will dispute my claim. Being entirely aware of the storm that my declaration was bound to precipitate, I waited until I was eighty recognizing that, if the heat of the uproar became too great, my advanced age coupled with an active libido would ensure that I was soon cooling my ardour in a hotter place. I also considered the decision carefully because, as the saying goes, there is no fool like an old fool.

When I told Adriana of my intent she cackled like an ancient whore and said, "You forget, old man, that I have known you for the better part of our two lives and that we once feasted together on Passion Mountain. If my memory is not riding a lame horse the feast turned out to be a snack with damp crackers and stale cheese. Perhaps you are the greatest lover of last Tuesday."

I chose to ignore this unkind remark, attributing it to the emotion of jealousy which Adriana had surely experienced in large quantity long ago when I opted to bestow my affection on another who had exhibited a more delicate and less brassy nature.

Throughout these pages, the reader will observe that Adriana is more than happy to speak at length concerning the deficiencies she sees in both my appearance and my temperament. I do not deny any of these imperfections although they caused my pursuit of love to be a complex undertaking, similar to completing a doctorate without a research grant. Generally, I avoided the issue of my looks and personality by not requiring my partners to have the type of beauty that my male colleagues seem to think is necessary to achieve an orgasmic experience. Most of them spend their time chasing women instead of pursuing love which is a little like eating the cornflakes box for breakfast.

Adriana acquired the house next door from one of her former husbands, a prominent municipal administrator who enjoyed a reputation for unselfishly providing moral guidance to many of our less fortunate citizens. Adriana threatened to expose him after she obtained a photograph of him already exposed while he counselled a young lady of questionable repute. As she later explained, "Nowhere in the *Good Samaritan Manual* does it stipulate that one's trousers should be loose around one's ankles when performing a charitable act."

Our visit to Passion Mountain took place shortly after she became my neighbour. Though the event happened when I was young, I clearly demonstrated the efficiency for which I subsequently became famous. Even in those early days I instinctively recognized the importance of briskness in the bedroom. Adriana claims not to have enjoyed the experience but this is belied by the fact that she has repeatedly said it should have lasted longer.

She has refused to replay the venture even though I expressed sympathy for her inexperience. "Entering the ring with a champion does not make one proficient in the sport of boxing," I told her. "Similarly, our sharing a bed does not ensure that you would acquire my skill in the art of love."

Long ago I left the decade of my life when I felt I had to do things in order that I might have accomplishments when I passed on. I decided to forego accomplishments as being too strenuous and unnecessary for either my well-being or my legacy as I had observed that legacies were generally the illegitimate offspring of over-achievers and that having one would produce little lasting benefit to anybody other than those who would gain the most by my passing.

Having no descendants, I am at the very tip of the last branch of my family tree, alone except for a rag-tag assortment of kin. Though I'm the type of individual who wishes ill to no one, I would not necessarily intervene if all of my relatives were collected together, placed on an open raft and towed in front of a passing iceberg. In lieu of icebergs, when I wander away from this mortal sweetness, I intend to bestow on each a fair portion of my accumulated debt — there will be little to divide among those who have graced my life as lovers and confidantes, though each in her own manner sparked an electric flash across my libido. Apart from Adriana there is no one left with whom I can share an idle hour to reminisce and speak lies about the past. All of my male contemporaries have either died or taken up golf which is the same thing.

As my life has turned from deed to narrative it is necessary for me to draw import from past events, and as much malicious muttering has been uttered concerning these events, I intend to set the record straight. Therefore, please join me on the journey to discover the secrets of great love and let my legacy be this record from which I now propose to erase all zigs and zags.

❦

I was not always a penurious wastrel but was born into opulent circumstances: the only child in a moneyed family. My mother said that during her pregnancy she was confined to a suite on the second floor of our house. It was there that I was to be welcomed into the world by the country's finest obstetrician who was to be assisted by an experienced nurse. When the historic day arrived my mother was moved from her large bed to a birthing table that had been acquired for the occasion.

My entrance into this world did not come quickly. The doctor and the nurse filled the time of my mother's labour by drinking from a flask that he produced out of his black bag. Sometime later he abandoned his position at the end of the table. When mother turned her head, she discovered that he and the nurse had removed their clothing and moved to the bed. She later claimed that the distraction of watching them caused her to miss many of the preliminary events surrounding my birth. It was only when I became persistent about pushing my head into the daylight that I regained her awareness. Apparently I hovered there, torn between security and distress, between warm and bleak, between bliss and misery . . . until, fed up with my indecision, she gave one mighty push forcing me into pandemonium — the bed bouncing, the doctor grunting, the nurse screaming, my mother moaning and me wailing.

It is my belief that, in my case, the small portion of the human psyche that guides us all was clearly influenced by the amorous and boozy event that occurred during my introduction to this life and that my destiny was thus presaged.

I was raised in the white house that sits atop the hill overlooking the eastern edge of the city of Aguas Profundas. Though it is not the largest city in Centroamérica, many believe it is the most beautiful. You may be familiar with the house. It was built for my grandfather in the last century. He was a great orator and it has always been known as La Casa del Viento, the house of wind. It was a lonely place. I remember as a child wandering from room to room looking for someone to talk to. Occasionally I would get lost in some unfamiliar part of the house. Then I would curl up in a corner and sleep to escape my fear that I would never find my way back. As I got older I carried a piece of chalk with which I marked the hallways as I passed. This facilitated my return as I simply had to backtrack past the servants engaged in washing the walls. The house held few pleasant memories and I disposed of it soon after my parents passed away.

I disliked being an only child, a feeling that persisted through all the days of my youth and continued right up until the morning my father's will was read. For years I have suffered from a chronic disorder — an allergic reaction to making a living. My father's estate freed me of that burden, and until my relatives interfered I was able to pursue matters of the heart with few distractions.

A student of mathematics does not jump into the world of quadratic equations without first mastering basic axioms. Love must be approached in the same prudent manner. It is a more important study than physics or biology for it is, at once, both science and art. Far too long have those of my sex tackled the subject as if they were operating a large aircraft — pull this lever, press a pedal, push that button. It is no wonder that many fail to get off the runway. The task, then, is to devise a flight plan that will take all aspiring pilots soaring into uncharted rapture.

Some years ago it occurred to me that no study of love would be complete without a retrospective view from some of my former partners. I have always drifted on the surface of life inside a widening froth of memories and it was my hope that meeting previous lovers would help me dip beneath that surface. For the most part this was a satisfying experience and with the help of ex-paramours I happily reconstructed many of my romantic encounters. I confess that deep within the recesses of my remaining libido I harboured an ulterior motive — that at least one of these reunions would be with someone willing to adopt the role of intimate companion as we both creep toward our final destination.

My interest in the fair sex was first stimulated by an incident that occurred soon after I had completed the initial decade of my life. After this event, that part of me which had heretofore been used solely for urinary purposes began to demonstrate the talent that eventually led it to enjoy a splendid apprenticeship followed by an inspired career in its chosen profession. Occasionally it still displays flashes of its former brilliance.

I remember it like this morning's coffee. I was in our garden attempting to capture nature using paper and paints. Sunlight had spilled around the corner of the house and was busy drying the morning dew. A noisy kiskadee, perched near the top of a giant tulip tree, was criticizing my work.

I was deep in creative concentration when she appeared next to me. "Who are you and what are you doing in my garden?" I demanded.

"My name is Leticia. I'm staying with my aunt next door. What are *you* doing? How old are you? Do you like my new dress?"

"I'm reproducing nature in a manner not equalled since Van Gogh," I replied. "I'm eleven and no, I don't like your dress."

She laughed. "Your sunflowers are terrible. They look like runny eggs on a breakfast plate." She grabbed my masterpiece, tore it in half and ran away carrying the pieces.

I gave chase after being momentarily distracted by the sight of her new dress flying up to expose a tanned thigh. I caught her on the far side of the yard, pushed her to the ground and sat on her until she apologized.

Inspiration is neutral — neither rational nor irrational. Like a noxious relative it appears when least expected but, unlike toxic kin, it provides no clue as to the outcome of its presence. So it was that, sitting on Leticia, I made one of the important statements of my life — a statement momentous in its implication. "If you ever do that again," I said, "I'll pull down your panties."

Well, to remove some of the turns in the road and get straight to the parking lot — she did and I did!

The effect was electric. I can only equate it to losing a limb or being cured of a crippling disease by evangelical inspiration. Though the incident progressed no further and was essentially innocent, I instinctively knew that here in front of me, exposed behind the bougainvillea at the edge of our garden, was my Holy Grail, my passion, and my life's calling. Being an individual of single minded purpose I have never looked back.

Years later I tried to explain to Adriana how I felt in that garden. We were drinking brandy on her patio and swallows dipped around us flecked golden by the last rays of a dying sun. My explanation produced a sly snicker. "So, old man, what attracted you to the cathedral was not a spiritual quest," she said. "It was the shape of the door."

"But it is only through the door that one can hope to find the sacred on the inside," I protested.

She raised her eyebrows. "That only applies if one can distinguish a cathedral from a whorehouse," she said.

I saw nothing of Leticia for more than fifty years though I carried the memory of her through the decades and, although our encounter had been innocent, I always found it pleasant to envision what it would be like were we to meet as adults and pursue our previous activity to the conclusion reached in my imaginings.

What, you may ask, can be learned from this minor skirmish that occurred so long ago in the first inning of the game of love? At the time, very little. Only in the brittle light of advancing age and only after I retraced my steps and spoke to Leticia, who is a retired art critic, a world authority on Van Gogh, and who now lives in her aunt's house near Casa de Viento, did I glean some understanding from the incident.

I telephoned her and described my goal, explaining that even though our connection had been short-lived, I had been deeply affected. I was surprised that she remembered me. She agreed to meet over lunch and I spent the evening in laborious anticipation.

The next morning I awoke early and left for the Café Dos Lunas to prepare for the meeting. The owner, Don Emilio, makes the best *café corregido* in the city. I told him to add an extra shot of tequila and then drank three cups before Leticia arrived.

I placed my briefcase beside a garden table far from the English-speaking Amazon parrots that Don Emilio keeps caged for the amusement of his patrons. Even so, their strident obscenities were clearly audible as I ordered liqueurs. Leticia is a self-assured statuesque woman and her eyes twinkled as we reintroduced ourselves. "So did you become a famous artist?" she asked, although it was obvious that she knew the answer.

"Art . . . fart . . . private part," screamed one of the parrots.

"No," I said, "far from it. I've rarely touched a palette since our paths last crossed. The painting you destroyed was almost my last."

"Ram . . . damn . . . bearded clam." The second parrot was even louder than his mate.

Leticia raised her eyebrows. "They are noisy, aren't they? I'm sorry if I caused you to turn away from your calling."

"Oh, no! On the contrary, Leticia. You were the first inspiration of my life. Because of you I found my true vocation — the quest for love. You made me see that a woman's anatomy was far more interesting than canvas and paints. Later I realized that so was her psyche." I finished my liqueur and ordered a brandy.

"Cock-eyed bride . . . moustache ride." Someone had spent a lot of time training Don Emilio's birds.

Leticia rolled her eyes toward the parrots. "They're very crude. Do you come here often? . . . and why do you say that a woman's psyche is interesting?"

"Yes, I do come here often. Don Emilio's food is excellent. A woman's psyche is interesting because it's one of the few mysteries left. All of the other so-called mysteries are just problems to be solved. Women, their psyches and sex are mysteries to be lived — they can never be solved." I signalled for another brandy.

"Female . . . male . . . piece of tail." The parrots shrieked together.

Leticia frowned and put her hands over her ears. "Oh, shut up," she said.

It took a moment to realize she was talking to the parrots. "They can't understand you," I said.

She laughed. "I know. Maybe you're right. But isn't it frustrating to have mysteries you can't explain? Surely men are also mysteries, although I confess that I don't find them that interesting."

"Gawk . . . squawk . . . grab your cock."

Don Emilio came into the garden carrying a plate of mango and papaya. The parrots sensed lunch and my words carried across the garden in the sudden silence. "Oh no, Leticia. Men aren't mysteries. They're an open book and the first paragraph says, 'if you can't eat it, screw it or hit it with a golf club, grab a beer and turn the page'. There's a parody of an old English poem that speaks of men not loving without sex and of women refusing sex without love:

Jack and Jill went up the hill
To play an adult game.
Jack came down with a broken crown,
Jill needed love before she came.

They never tried the match again
The impasse was complete.
Jack could only love you see
If Jill was indiscreet.

Do you remember what happened after you ripped my painting the second time?"

"Yes I do," she answered.

"The sight of you naked set the direction of my life. I'm in your debt. Were it not for that incident I could have wasted my years. I might have become an engineer, a lawyer or, God forbid, a cleric. Thank you for not telling your aunt."

I pointed to her glass. "Are you ready for another?"

"No thanks, but you go ahead."

I waved at Don Emilio.

Leticia's smile returned. "But you obviously didn't understand then, and I'm afraid you still don't. I would never have told. I liked you. I wanted you to do what you did and I was disappointed when you didn't pursue the matter. I ripped your painting to provoke you. I had formulated no plan but what transpired followed the oldest blueprint in the world."

"Aha, Leticia. You make my point. Women are so mysterious they don't even understand themselves."

She sipped her anisette. "You're right. There were many things I didn't understand. I had not yet developed the knowledge that sex was bad or alternatively, that it was a precious thing. But somehow I sensed it was a commodity and like any commodity it had power — the power of being desired. Even grown men rarely understand that. They gain their power from physical aggression and, occasionally, violence. Neither is a commodity and usually neither is desired. Therefore a man's version of power is a puny thing — a gun that, when fired, produces a flag that says, 'bang'. It's ironic that I, a female, used physical aggression to gain your attention."

"You are making yourself sound like a whore," I said. Her face went out of focus. "Surely you overstate the shituation." My tongue was having difficulty placing letters in the correct location.

"Maybe," she answered. "I was too young to have received the message that the world sends to all women — that their bodies are less than ideal — and so I had not yet created the inhibitions that would ultimately cause me to believe that shame and self-loathing are a permanent part of the female identity. Even at that age I instinctively tendered sex for affection or, at least, the *interest* I mistook for affection."

She raised her glass and continued. "I may have started my sex life as a young offender but I became a parole officer. That's a promotion given to all women when they learn that the so-called imperfections of a body are just traces of life and not the progenitors of shame or self-loathing."

I reached for my glass to return her salute, but mis-triangulated and knocked it from the table. It didn't break. I bent to retrieve it and paused beneath the table to relish an unfamiliar stirring in my loins. Leticia's sheer nylons, exposed to mid thigh, were inches from my face. *Now*, I thought, *now*! I dropped my glass again, reached for my briefcase, opened it, and extracted a small painting.

"What's this?" she asked.

"A field of shunflowers . . . painted yesterday."

"Why?"

"A memento . . . 'membrance of good times. Be so kind . . . rip it in half."

"Why?" she asked again.

I was fully aroused. "Tear it . . . more interesting than before." I held out the painting.

Her face flushed. "Are you crazy? You want to re-create fifty years ago . . . or is this a ridiculous joke?"

I staggered as I stood up. "Do it, Leticia. Iss bookend to our lifes."

"This is as vulgar as the parrots." She looked at my erection. "I don't want to be part of an old drunk's wet dream. You'll have to find another playmate . . . and . . . " She grabbed the painting and tore it in half. "You'll have to find another piece of flowery pornography."

"Oh Lord and Mother of God! Thank you, Leticia."

She stared at me. "Is your life so lacking that you play kid's games? I feel sorry for you."

Staggering, I took my leave of Leticia. I knew that, behind her anger and pity, she desired me but I sensed the attraction was not strong. If there is one thing I know, it is that the pursuit of an unwilling woman, while much romanticized, is fraught with diminishing returns, much like walking up a down escalator or hiking around the block to visit the house next door. Besides, her anger had distracted me and while my motive was research, I had also hoped for a delightful afternoon revisiting the site of my first sight — a fantasy that reached its climax and evaporated the moment she tore my painting.

Days later, seated on Adriana's patio, I tried to convey my frustration. "The reality is not like the imagination," I said. "I'm disappointed."

"But, old man, you must know that what you call mystery is really illusion — it and disappointment are the true attributes of love. For example, the image of a man's organ that I carried in my head was not a small organ . . . until I met you. Your shorts should carry the warning, 'contents may cause drowsiness'."

"You're wrong, my peevish puzzle. Love doesn't care about size . . . and it's more than an image in the head — there's thought involved."

"I agree," she said. "Perhaps it depends on which head you're using when you do your thinking."

Sometimes Adriana's insults sting and I consider putting a stop to our daily encounters. However, I immediately relent when I contemplate the sorrow that she would surely feel were she forced to go through life without me.

"You're also wrong about illusion," I said. "My life in the service of love has taught me that women are indeed enigmatic, but like all things that perplex they conceal the truth of their own mystery. A real lover never swings for home runs — always for the stars — since love lies beyond lust and illusion. Truth becomes visible because genuine passion demands that lovers hide nothing from each other."

Adriana gave me a rueful smile. "I wish it were that simple," she said. "A man's attention only means there's pressure in his loins. You're also wrong about home runs. A man wants grand slams. A woman, on the other hand, recognizes that the game is composed of running, hitting, fielding and walks. She knows it also includes strikeouts which she does not consider failures."

She smirked at her own wit. I said goodnight and made my way home to bed where I lay awake wondering why we spend so much time worrying about the future when contemplating the mysteries of the past may occasionally provide insight or a lesson.

And the lesson . . . there are two. The first is, the search for love may owe its genesis to a confused preoccupation with anatomy, and the second is that attraction may disguise itself as aggression, perhaps the modern offspring of an ancient mating ritual. The corollary is that simulating the past may stimulate the present even if the result is the destruction of painted sunflowers that resemble runny eggs.

My Albatross

OUR CITY ORIGINATED YEARS AGO WHEN the area was settled by a few gentlemen who were assigned to the new world frontier by their wealthy families because they lacked the intellectual accoutrements to participate in enterprises at home. Referring to what has come to be known as the Principle of Poor Progenitors, a few cynical newcomers have speculated that everything that has happened since can be traced to both the leadership and the brains of these original pathfinders.

My parents met during the holiday that celebrates the death of Bartolomé Albatross, one of these early pioneers and the first mayor of our town, who in 1792 had been masticated to death by a herd of wild cows as he laid the first cobble for a new road in what was then a large pasture. The road was to become the rain-soaked street on which Papa's car skidded and failed to stop when my mother raced into his path in pursuit of a street dog. The dog had stolen a chicken she was carrying home for a special family dinner, always held on the day of the festival that honours the martyrdom of Mayor Albatross. She was sixteen and beautiful, and my father was enamoured long before they arrived at the clinic where he paid to have her fractured ankle treated. Later he drove her home and later still, after a courtship that was opposed by his parents, they were married. Until her dying day my mother maintained that Papa owed her the price of the chicken because she had been gaining on the dog when his car crashed into her.

§

The original incident with Leticia had aroused my sleeping bantam-weight from hibernation and it was therefore inevitable that I embark on the quest that has been the preoccupation of males through history — the search for a female willing to explore and to be explored. Along the way I learned that, like new continents, every woman is different and that, unlike Cortez who burned his ships at Veracruz, would-be lovers must never enter uncharted territory without an adequate escape route. What I didn't realize was that females, since the dawn of upright men, have engaged in exploratory journeys of their own albeit with slightly different goals and methodologies.

By the time I was well into the second decade of my life I was aware of many of the tricks employed by both sexes in the search for love: the pretended disdain shown by a lady that causes a suitor to trip over his own feet while scurrying back and forth between panic and lust; the declarations of undying love sworn by a male whose frantic goal is the release of corralled ejaculate; the exaggerated pain experienced by a man with a slivered posterior acquired while straddling the fence that separates passion from feigned indifference; the moans of a female orgasmically anticipating the envious coos of girlfriends as they drool over her new engagement ring.

Adolescence brought exciting changes to my life, not the least of which was a requirement for more frequent changes . . . of my sheets. I was fifteen when I finally entered the cathedral. After much fumbling with pubescent girls I was fortunate enough to encounter a willing lady who was three times my age and who, along with her husband, leased the villa next door to ours in the small resort town of Puerto Paraiso. Her name was Mimi Albatross and her husband Alvin was a direct descendant of our first mayor. Though they lived in New York, Alvin had been raised in our city and was a long-time friend of my father. The Albatrosses were well-moneyed and it was rumoured that they had acquired much of their wealth as a result of his activities in organized crime.

One evening I accompanied my parents to a party that Mrs. Albatross threw to celebrate her husband's forty-fifth birthday. I attended because I was broke and unable to participate in other activities. Father believed that denying me money or an allowance of any kind would stiffen my back and lead me to the strength of character needed to accomplish the goals that he planned on setting for me.

There was no one of my age in attendance, so to alleviate the queasiness caused by teen boredom I went exploring. I soon found myself in the cellar, alone with Mr. Albatross's wine collection.

For more years than I care to remember the dark cloud of alcohol hovered over my life. It's probable that the cloud was formed that night in the dim light of the Albatross cellar.

I was exploring my second bottle of Chateau Margaux, marvelling at how the first had washed away my boredom, when voices appeared at the top of the stairs. I set the bottle on the floor and hid behind the wine rack. From my vantage point in the darkness I peered between the shelves and saw Mr. Albatross coming down the stairs closely followed by Señora Adora Reyes, my school principal.

Señora Reyes was giggling. "I've heard of etchings, Alvin, but you're the first to ask me into his cellar to view a wine collection."

Mr. Albatross didn't answer but grasped her around the waist and kissed her. They immediately engaged in such frantic groping that a less astute individual than myself might have mistakenly concluded that they were wrestling. It continued until Señora Reyes stepped back and said, "Let me do it."

She raised her dress, pushed down a pair of white frilly panties, lifted her foot to step free and stumbled against the shelves. I was forced to react quickly to keep them from falling and exposing my presence.

Then, the señora turned and looked at me. I almost said hello before I realized that her eyes couldn't penetrate the inky murk behind the shelves. She bent over and braced herself as Mr. Albatross pushed from behind. I watched both their faces from the gloom as they began a knee knocking rhythm which caused the señora to yelp, Mr. Albatross to utter deep guttural sounds and the bottles to rattle.

Somewhere in mid-knock, he moved his foot and tipped the Margaux that I hadn't finished exploring. It clattered and gurgled as wine splashed around their feet. After a few minutes Mr. Albatross emitted a great final grunt and the señora sighed, "Oh no, are you finished already, Alvin?" He grunted again, backed up and zipped his pants.

They climbed the stairs and I was left alone with the two empty bottles and Señora Reyes' underwear. I opened another Margaux, put the panties in my pocket, lurched up the stairs and let myself into the party.

Mr. Albatross was standing by his birthday cake. The wine bent my logic — here was a wealthy man and I had the means to acquire some of that wealth. I adopted a sophisticated swagger and sauntered over.

"Hello Alvin." I reached out, stumbled, lost my balance and plunged my hand through the cake as I tried to prevent a dive into the punch bowl.

Mr. Albatross stepped back. "Careful, young man. My wife baked that herself."

"Forget it. I'll buy you another." I licked icing from my hand and washed it down with Margaux.

He grinned. "It may take a while. From what I hear, your father doesn't give you any money . . . and there *are* wine glasses at the bar, Alberto."

"I don't need his charity. I'll soon have lots of money."

"Oh," said Mr. Albatross, "and how will that come about?"

"You're going to give it to me, Alvin." Though I was drunk, I remember a distinct feeling that I wasn't being particularly clever.

Mr. Albatross's grin decreased to a tight smile. "Why should I do that?"

"Because I have something for sale that you want."

"What's that?"

"These." I pulled Señora Reyes' panties from my pocket.

"Put those away, you idiot." He moved in front of me so that the panties were not visible to the rest of the room. "Give them to me!"

"Oh no, Alvin. Not 'til I get paid." I pushed the flimsy evidence back into my pocket.

"We'll discuss this later, you little snot." He pulled back his jacket, far enough to reveal a gun in a holster below his left armpit. "Now, get those out of here." He gestured at my pocket.

He's going to kill me, I thought. But my mind was marching to the Margaux and it turned to the question, *How much money should I demand?*

Hours later, I was still pondering though some of the wine-effects had dissipated. The party was a success. After our conversation, Mr. Albatross had celebrated to the extent that he was snoring loudly on a sofa by the time guests started to leave. Mrs. Albatross asked me to stay to help get him up to the bedroom. I was about to flee when she clumped back from saying goodbye to the last guests.

I felt her breath on my neck and she reached around and grabbed that part of my anatomy that I had begun to fear was going to spend much of its life dependant on unemployment insurance. I knew immediately that she had drunk too much tequila — we were in plain view should Mr. Albatross choose to open his eyes. I remembered the gun and determined to resist. "Please don't," I whispered. "What if Mr. Albatross should wake up?"

Though her action had produced a near-instant reaction, I gritted my teeth and summoned my willpower. "I'm resolved to stand firm," I said.

Her grip tightened. "Oh . . . you are!" she said. "And you *are* making a point."

The point I was making seemed to encourage her. In seconds, I was completely exposed and quite beyond a rational response, not that I would have been able to control any response, rational or otherwise. My immediate future was in Mrs. Albatross's hands.

Suddenly she let go, turned and bent over a table, simultaneously raising her dress so that I was afforded a view not only of the cathedral but of the surrounding landscape which rivalled the expanse of a small country.

"Go ahead," she said. "Fulfill your heart's desire."

At that moment Mr. Albatross spluttered and adjusted himself on the sofa. The interruption spurred Mrs. Albatross to a new height of aggression. She reached behind and grabbed me. "Bring that hardened resolve here," she said.

I have never been a religious man but if circumstances conspire to lead me to a cathedral I respond to the sanctity of the place by adopting a calm and contemplative attitude. Not so that first time. That encounter produced an internal storm of such intensity that most of the region was flooded before I reached the front steps. Mrs. Albatross proved patient, however, and I was soon awash in as great a spiritual tempest as it's possible to experience and still remain on this side of heaven's portal. Or at least as great an experience as it's possible to have with a two hundred pound lady whose husband is snoring right behind you.

. . . Or, was snoring right behind me. Silence! I turned my head. Mr. Albatross's eyes were open and he was reaching inside his jacket. "I'll shoot you, you horny little bastard," he said.

I bolted for the door and slept the night under a small bridge in a wet ditch.

Generations later, Adriana proved neither understanding nor sympathetic.

"What happened? Why are you still alive to torment me? Have you been hiding all your life?"

"The Albatrosses left a few days later or I'd still be under the bridge. Lucky for me, Alvin died of an allergic reaction to piano wire before his next scheduled visit to Puerto Paraiso. He was found floating in a lake in upstate New York."

"So you escaped scott free?"

"No I didn't. Before he left he told Senora Reyes about my spying and there were some major educational repercussions. I'll tell you about them another time."

"What about Mimi Albatross? Did you see her again? With that swiftness you should have raced at the Olympics, although you probably would have been disqualified for prematurely leaving the starting blocks. Did you learn anything, old man, or was it just a swallow of life that you gulped without tasting?" She threw this over her shoulder as she marched across her patio to retrieve more brandy for what has evolved into our daily ritual of insults and alcohol. I refrained from commenting on the intriguing picture her buttocks made as each undulated, amply and separately, under her light summer dress reminding me of two bear cubs wrestling in a sack.

Learn anything? No, I hadn't, and to learn something retroactively it is necessary to delve into Mimi Albatross' motivation. Of course, she is also dead so ascribing motive to her actions is largely speculation.

The old villa was still there, a ruin sitting high on a finger of land that jutted far into the sea. It simultaneously provided a magnificent view and a feeling of anxiety — a feeling inspired by the implied vulnerability of standing with an unpredictable ocean on three sides. What *was* her motivation? Why me? Why does a middle aged woman choose to have a copulatory moment with someone who is at an age where the hormones gushing through his body have displaced all common sense? Who knows the aetiology of sex?

I turned and put my back to the mysteries hiding beyond a placid horizon and faced the mysteries of my memory. While it's true that older women don't have time for gymnastics of the head, it still required either courage or a full suitcase of desperation for Mimi Albatross to throw caution aside and make the statement she did — even if that statement was symbolic and only to herself.

❦

When I proffered these speculations to Adriana she snorted and said, "Your glasses are fogged by the temperature difference between reality and your imagination, old man. Are you so blind as to think that the only view of something is from where you're standing? What divine dictate says that a woman has to see sex or love or relationships through your spectacles? Know that the plot for love may be complex but the plot for sex alone is simple and straightforward."

Her sharp tone offended me. "You underestimate me, my large lump of loveliness. I realize it's not necessary for a woman to believe that sex is a cherished thing, connected only to love."

"You do, do you? That *is* a breakthrough! Do you also know that women often want sex just for fun? There is no statute that says a woman cannot enjoy a good romp once in awhile. What makes you think that men are the only creatures congenitally incapable of fidelity? At one time or another we all expose our animal nature. Men become tomcats, beaver chasers, or horndogs. Women turn into lust bunnies, sex kittens, or bitches in heat. It's good to occasionally separate emotion and lust . . . and we all know that sometimes monogamy is boring."

"But, listen to me," I protested.

She didn't hear.

"Men get their feelings through sex," she said, "and women usually get sex through their feelings. But, there are times when the reverse is true, even if the sex is with a hormonally brain-damaged fifteen-year-old who has no chance of recovery."

She drained her glass and went into the house. I rationed my brandy and gazed at the night sky until a star fell into the city. I was certain that it wasn't pleasure that Mimi Albatross searched for that night, and according to Adrianna she wasn't making a statement. What *was* she after? Was it simply the unfamiliar?

Of course, speculation aside, I *had* learned something. It dawned on me that the intensity of the experience and the feelings produced would not have varied one iota had the lady involved been Cleopatra or a Hollywood legend. The lesson then is that the level of ecstasy produced by an erotic experience is not affected by the fame or beauty of the participants, so one who would be a lover must forget stereotypes and concentrate solely on the pleasure of the moment. After all, the world is a better place following an orgasm.

School Days

WE HAD STOPPED FOR LUNCH AT a small restaurant near Plaza Bugambillias. I blocked out Adriana's prattle by concentrating my attention on three pictures hanging in the centre of the white stucco wall: a faded print of a marching school band, a watercolour of an old boat tied to the pier at the end of the malecon and a recent photo of the owner's wife preparing a culinary masterpiece in a cluttered kitchen. Faded red flowers stencilled onto a painted green vine surrounded the pictures and then rambled around a door, open to a private dining area in the rear of the restaurant.

Adriana's voice rose to blur the pictures. "You are like a puppy that outruns its own legs," she said. "You're way ahead of yourself and you're about to fall flat on your face."

"What do you mean, oh faded flower of painted pulchritude?"

"You have already informed your reader, should you be so fortunate as to get one, how you sneaked up the backstairs on your first visit to a cathedral. You have said little of what went before. What of your days in school? You must enlighten us on how someone can spend his entire youth getting educated and still learn nothing."

She picked up the salt and pepper shakers which were topped up with rice kernels to capture moisture during the wet season, and began to methodically cover her salad. I redialled my gaze to the shelf above Adriana's head — a shelf shared by a small ceramic cactus and a metal figurine of a man with a large hat lunging after, but failing to tackle a runaway rooster. "You're absolutely right, my crowing cutie. I have gotten ahead of myself. Let me repair that situation."

※

After a long and lonely childhood I reached the age where my behaviour became intolerable and my parents deemed that I was old enough to begin my formal education. It was my mother's wish that I be sent to a public school though my father expressed misgivings. He said that with his wealth there was no need for me to risk pollution by associating with the rabble spawned by his inferiors. My mother arched her back and stuck out her chin. "I'm part of that rabble and I may have married beneath myself," she said. "If public school was good enough for me, it's certainly good enough for my offspring." The following day I was enrolled as a beginner at Albatross Public Elementary School.

It was my fate to start academic life under the tutelage of Señora Camila Gutierrez, a stern and haughty matron who felt that the large amount of prestige attached to my family name had to be diluted by daily applications of a leather strap. "It's required to mould your character," she said. "Now, bend over."

Fortunately for my nether region and unfortunately for my character, after exactly one year of moulding, Señora Gutierrez was recruited by the military to teach hand-to-hand combat to army commandos. She was succeeded by a number of men and women, good teachers all, who supplied me with the foundation on which I built the figurative skyscraper, currently emblazoned with dignity and old age, which the world now knows as a great lover.

I proved adept and the foundation was well under construction by the time I reached adolescence. I had not forgotten the episode with Leticia and as I navigated through puberty, my boat sailing merrily along on an ocean of wet dreams, I began to experience an embarrassing and uncontrollable phenomenon. It became necessary for me to hold my book bag in front of me at all times. At first my parents were pleased when I carried my homework to church and to the beach. They saw it as evidence that I loved learning and that I was maturing into someone who took his studies seriously. They were soon disappointed.

I began to ignore algebra and literature in favour of intoxicating eyes and blossoming breasts, and my academic life started to founder in a sea of right-handed fantasy.

It was at this time that Señora Reyes decided to repay my attempt to blackmail Alvin Albatross. She sent my parents a special report card outlining my failures both in and out of class. The report stated that my social skills were at the same level as a psychopathic scorpion, that my athletic ability was similar to that of a dismembered sloth and that I had the same academic potential as body lice. She recommended that I leave school and begin an apprenticeship at a faraway zoo, either cleaning cages or as an exhibit.

My father initiated an 'I told you so' campaign and I was soon disengaged from public school in favour of education at home with private tutors. The change of venue and the episode with Mimi Albatross did not impair my imagination. By the time I was sixteen my heart ached for every girl I met. Those that held me close while pushing their tongues doggedly against the back of my throat held an exalted place in my fantasy, and those who continued kissing while I enthusiastically shoved my hand down their pants I placed on a pedestal so high they qualified for pubescent sainthood. I believed I loved and because I believed it, I did.

Walking home from one of those sweaty excruciating sessions, the night air cooling my face, the leaves turning on the trees and whispering to a pregnant moon, tasting the air filled with the smell of desert lavender and sweet acacia, it was love just as I believed. No Juliet was ever loved more than those adolescent girls whom I touched and who touched me with all the yearning that juvenile hormones can manufacture and squeeze into an evening. The ecstasy of those nights, the excitement of discovery, the gratitude, the tenderness, the love — together created an intense joy that seared itself into each step in a way that no adult romance has ever done.

Those nights and the days with my teachers are twinned in my memory. The exhilaration of the evening translated into a joy of learning such that new knowledge became a daytime proxy for night-time pleasure.

One of my first tutors was Antoine Cabbage, a French scholar and expert on the human situation, who in a lifetime of research had discovered correlations between the medical conditions that affect human beings and the behaviour that precipitates those conditions. Between lectures on philosophy and classical history, he passed on much of the wisdom that he had garnered in fifty years of observation and thinking.

His grand theory stated that our innermost thoughts and desires lead to various behaviours and that it is possible to deconstruct those behaviours so that they provide insight into a person's future. He called the first part of his theory Cabbage's Leap into Prediction which popularly became known as CLIP.

The theory went on to state that the behaviours and actions generated by a person's thoughts and desires lead to various conditions and afflictions, many of which cause misery. He called the second part of his theory Cabbage's Law of Pain or CLOP. "Using CLIP-CLOP I can infer causation so that it's possible to say which human behaviour causes what medical condition," he told me.

He eschewed tired old saws such as smoking stunts growth, masturbation leads to poor eyesight, sweets cause acne and unnatural sex practices promote baldness. "They all mean nothing," he said. "No research has ever backed them up. I use more sophisticated models that will be made explicit in my book." He had been writing a medical text for over thirty years.

Some of his conclusions were complex and startling, so he took pains to ensure I understood. "My research has shown that chronic nose-picking leads to incontinence," he said. "And it's a well known fact that infidelity causes hair loss. It therefore follows that one should not occupy a seat on the bus next to a bald adulterer who is picking his nose."

I expressed amazement, but not enough to remind him that I was supposed to be studying Italian Renaissance history.

"That's just the beginning," he said. "I have found that self-abuse causes dwarfism and obesity in young men and old ladies. In all others, self-abuse causes excessive growth and anorexia. Therefore all tall, short, thin and fat people have written their own biographies, so-to-speak."

In one semester at a well known university, he had set the academic world on fire by announcing that burping in public while young precipitates blindness in old age, wiping one's nose on one's sleeve causes paranoid schizophrenia and that cheating in cards brings on the flu while cheating on one's spouse gives rise to migraine headaches.

Over and over he warned all who would listen, "Sex, in any form is lethal. It triggers heart attacks and cancer. Just consider that almost 100% of adults who die from heart attacks or cancer have, at one time or another, practiced sex."

Notwithstanding the effort he put into his research, Professor Cabbage had detractors, some of whom were so unkind as to refer to his work as CLIP-CLOP clap-trap. These unkind aspersions simply made him work harder. "CLIP-CLOP is not clap-trap," he used to say. "They're all envious. If they had read my last paper they would know that envy and jealousy beget venereal disease. They may not fry in hell, but they'll certainly burn when they urinate."

For years he had wrestled with the fact that on average every human being has one breast and one testicle. His breakthrough was memorable. He came into the room, red-eyed from lack of sleep. "I have it," he said. "Consider the following: It's a fact that only one testicle is necessary for procreation, and it's also a fact that one breast is indeed sufficient to feed a normal baby. Therefore every woman has one unneeded breast and every man, an extraneous testicle. Obviously the human body carries around pieces it doesn't require. Because God is efficient and would never give parts to humans that they don't need, the extras must have been placed on our bodies by the Devil . . . and because these extra bits are naughty, they have an innate ability to assist in arousal. It follows that Satan has placed them on us in an effort to get men and women to increase sexual activity."

"More sex doesn't sound bad," I said.

He gave me a pitying look. "Remember, once humans engage in sex, it's a very short step into the grave. The only way out of the dilemma is to abstain. Then one can die of old age which is the only human affliction that's manufactured by God. He has provided it so that we can all go to heaven. It's not difficult. With one exception, I've abstained for over seventy years."

Notwithstanding his one exception, Professor Cabbage had made it to old age and it wasn't long until a dwindling supply of mental resources forced his retirement. He died a few years later and I'm sure he has an exalted place in heaven. Occasionally he enters one of my recurring dreams. In it he is sitting next to God observing the afflictions that caused the demise of the persons whose souls are slowly making their way toward the celestial gate. Before each arrives the professor does a calculation and informs God of the result. Then God makes the ultimate decision and Professor Cabbage smiles, secure in the knowledge that CLIP-CLOP is not clap-trap.

We had progressed from the restaurant to Adriana's patio. The afternoon heat had refused to retreat before an early evening moon and Adriana was fanning herself with a magazine. "Your story explains some of your peculiarities," she said. "However, studying under the professor doesn't account for all of your less-desirable characteristics. Surely you must have had other influences besides Professor Cabbage."

The heat had caused my shirt to stick to my back. I was uncomfortable and Adriana's words irritated me. "Yes I did, my sweaty señora. If you can control your outbursts, I'll tell you."

Professor Cabbage was replaced by a series of instructors, each of whom was interesting and each of whom taught me well, but who, upon leaving my father's employ, immediately erased themselves from my memory. That is, until my last tutor, Philomena Philander, age twenty-one. She had been hired specifically to teach me Latin.

Please don't misunderstand. Those who know me now may not realize that there was a time when I did not speak many languages. Now, I am a master. I have, in addition to vigorous French, a small smattering of Chinese, a tiny dab of Armenian and some strikingly apologetic Canadian.

Philomena was well-educated but unemployed due to her marriage to Don Rodolfo, a sixty-year-old man who felt she should be at home to look after his every need. She became my tutor only because of a debt owed to my father by Don Rodolfo. Gypsy haired, incandescent, and sybaritic, her eyes were molten and she moved with the quivering wildness of a caged jaguar which caused her clothing to float about her body and rustle with erotic implication.

I was obsessed from the moment I saw her. Previous loves faded from my mental album as quickly and quietly as morning dew fades from grass. My father introduced us. She looked through me and spoke only to him. "Don't worry, señor. He'll be speaking Latin like a native in no time."

My father grinned as he left the room. "I'm sure he will," he said.

I soon discovered that I didn't exist. Philomena and I were alone during my lessons but when she talked she spoke past me and she never expected an answer. It was like I was invisible. Whenever she turned away, I strained to see my image in the glass on the door to prove that I was really there, but I appeared as a shadow with no more identity than a shapeless smudge.

Flailing helplessly and miserably in a vat of intense longing, I desired beyond excess. Foolish me, I now know that desire creates first anxiety and then lunacy. It's the reason women become calculating, neurotic, and self-destructive — why they get face-lifts, pierce their nipples, and dye their hair. It makes men obsessive, mean, and uncompromising. It's why they also get face-lifts, pierce their nipples, and dye their hair.

As time passed, even my shadow disappeared from the door taking my self-esteem with it. I began to talk and behave in the manner that I thought others expected. I lost all will and believed myself inferior. Soon, like a soft chair, I started to take on the shape of the last person to sit on me. Yearning and torment became my daily bread and I came to feel that there was no reason to continue on this earth.

One day, near the low point of my existence, through the mist of my misery, I glimpsed the shape of my salvation. Philomena wrote Julius Caesar's famous phrase, *veni, vidi, vici* on the blackboard. She said it was a well known tongue twister which meant 'the venerable vicar's vinegar'. She then followed with *amo, amas, amen*, which she translated as 'I love, you love, the end'. I sensed that she knew little Latin. The fog started to lift and as it gained altitude, I regained some of my confidence. "Have you *ever* studied Latin?" I asked.

Immediately, she began to cry. Soon her head was on my shoulder, tears staining my shirt as she confessed. She had been suffocating in her house and in her marriage. Claiming to know Latin was her escape. Her aloofness was a ruse, a disguise that she donned to keep me ignorant and so remain employed. The pressure of maintaining the charade had taken her to the edge and my question had pushed her over. The mornings spent teaching me were the only reason she was sane. Now she would be forced back to a bleak house and a bleaker marriage. I hugged her and did my best to console her, promising that her secret was safe.

My father began the annoying habit of periodically quizzing me on what I was learning. In order to hide the fact that Philomena knew no Latin, I started to study in earnest. We became co-conspirators and learned together. I began to pass his surprise tests with flying colours and, pleased, he increased her salary.

Every morning we were left alone and eventually the inevitable happened. One day Philomena wrote *si vis amari ama* on the board and then began pacing back and forth. I calculated that the phrase meant 'if you want to be loved, then love', and repeated it out loud. She stopped in front of me. "Well, do you?" she asked.

"Do I what?"

"Do you want to be loved?"

At first I didn't understand. I put down my pen. Then a great hope filled me and the next thing I knew we were out of control, kissing exponentially. Her body and my pent-up response came together in a radiant flare that left my knees weak and gave the room a surreal quality. There is no image that precisely portrays what happened. The best would be lying with eyes closed in the centre of a symphonic orchestra while music, dressed in shimmering colours, washes over you as the conductor lures dulcet note after dulcet note from each surrounding instrument until, at the crescendo, the music enters your body to become the organ with which you taste, feel, smell, hear and see. No nerve remains untouched. You vibrate in ecstatic harmony until every emotion coalesces into one enormous explosion.

That was our lovemaking. We were like gigantic balloons filled with beauty that burst daily to envelop us in layer upon layer of enchantment. It became our habit each morning to rush into each other's arms and begin anew the cycle of ardour that we had created. We played and replayed the possibilities of sensual delight. We created new techniques of gratification. We danced naked and memorized each others' bodies. We whispered, then shouted our secrets and intimate thoughts. We relished our complicity and ignored the risk of an unlocked door, forgetting the world, my parents, her husband, and my lessons. In this blissful state, we slipped through weeks until one day, without the encumbrance of clothing, we were experimenting with new methods of arousal by trying all the permutations of *veni, vidi, vici*, when I looked up to see my father and Don Rodolfo standing in the doorway. In the ensuing confusion, Philomena mistakenly put on my trousers which left me with no alternative but to cover my bare essentials by wrestling myself into her tiny dress while I explained that acting out the Latin phrases helped me retain them in my memory.

My explanation was dismissed and so was Philomena. We were warned never to see each other again. Of course, for someone as in love as I, that was impossible. That very evening, I stole from the house and made my way to Philomena's. Keeping to the shadows I tossed pebbles at the only lighted window. Soon the front door opened and Don Rodolfo stepped out carrying a shotgun. "I have been expecting you," he said. "Philomena is not here. I have sent her to live with the nuns at a mission that is so far away that you will never find her. She will not return until she regains her sanity. Now, go home and do not bother me again."

I could not believe it. I felt as though my heart were ripped from my chest and hurled into my stomach. A hundred devils with tiny hammers began pounding my brain. Much as I begged, Don Rodolfo would not reveal the name of the mission. Instead, he promised to reveal the contents of his shotgun if I did not go.

I know that it is impossible to kill passion by arguing against it. Nevertheless, an argument that contains buckshot is a powerful persuader. I ran home convinced that life, for me, was over. There I pined, feeding my sorrow with brandy stolen from my father's liquor cupboard, and rarely leaving my room until it came time for me to go to university.

❧

It was dark on the patio but I'm sure I saw a tear on Adriana's cheek. "It's a heartbreaking tale you spin, my naked nincompoop," she said. "The story of young love ripped asunder is always sad, although sometimes a little melodramatic. What did you do?"

"Nothing at first. I knew I would die. How could I not? My one true love was torn away. How could I ever desire another?"

"You were probably surprised at how easy it was. Are you sure Philomena didn't come to your house with low expectations and leave disappointed? Did you ever see her again? Did she return to Don Rodolfo?"

"No, my curious crone. Don Rodolfo died and she never returned. I didn't see her again until recently when I attended a lecture on dead languages given by a visiting professor. When the professor entered the theatre, I immediately recognized her as Philomena. After her talk, I introduced myself but she did not seem pleased to see me."

❧

"It's been a very long time," she said. You know I waited months for you to come to the mission for me. I was watched twenty-four hours a day. When I finally reconciled myself to the knowledge that you weren't coming, I devised my own plan to escape."

"What did you do?" I asked.

"I was assigned to work planting a vegetable garden. I'm quite artistic so I arranged my garden in a manner that when the vegetables grew they formed an image that could be viewed from a small hill behind the chapel."

"What kind of an image?"

"An image of our Lord. It caused quite a stir. You may recall, it was written up in the press all over the country."

"I didn't know that was you," I said.

"The garden was termed a miracle and it wasn't long until the faithful from all over the world arrived to view the image, although by then it was not exactly as I had designed it."

"What do you mean, not as you designed it? Was there divine intervention while the garden was growing?"

"Not exactly. It was Mother Superior who intervened. She said the image was too realistic, so she cut out the cucumber vine."

"I see. Perhaps her action was divinely inspired. How did you escape?"

"It was easy. In the confusion created by thousands of supplicants, I simply walked away."

"Tell me the rest," I said. "What did you do?"

"At that time I still believed I loved you, but I didn't return because it was necessary for our relationship to end. We could not give up our lives for each other, and I could no longer live with an old man who wanted me only for work. I didn't know that Don Rodolfo was dead. My time at the mission allowed me to think and my eyes had opened to the possibilities in life."

"But we loved each other."

"What I had called love was a desperate attempt to become real, to escape. My life had dipped to the point that when I looked in a mirror, I could not recognize the person looking back. The day my image disappeared was the day I first made love with you. Our sex had a practical aspect. It kept me in touch with reality. I truly think that I was close to vanishing completely."

I felt my knees weaken as she cut away the illusion that had coated my self-portrait for so many years. "You mean that you made love only to maintain your equilibrium — that you had no feelings for me?"

"Not at all. I said our affair had a practical purpose. I didn't say that I was aware of that purpose. At the time I sincerely felt that I loved you. Our sex was an expression of that love and, most important, it was also pleasure. It's not unlike reading a good book. We do it for pleasure but it also has the practical purpose of increasing our knowledge."

"What made you step back from the edge?" I asked. "Surely it was more than a vegetable garden."

"Oh, yes. It happened when the cover was lifted from our subterfuge. Only after we were caught and there was nothing left to hide, did I realize that I didn't need my family's, my husband's or anyone else's approval. You were my escape and for that I thank you, but I became real only after I was able to make my own choices."

"How did you live? Did you get a job?"

"Although Latin was not my strength, I was educated. I had a relative who helped. I returned to university and worked hard. Eventually I added dead languages to my resumé, just below dead marriages and dead memories. But enough about me. What did you do? Did it take time to forget me? Did you get another tutor?"

"There was no other tutor and yes, it took time. After a few isolated days I soon realized that I would do the world no good confined to my room so I wrote the entrance exams for university. I could not pine away the rest of my life. Back to you. Did you re-marry? Do you have a family? Did you find love?"

"Yes to all. I found a man who was secure enough to be my equal. It was difficult because my anguish had caused me to stereotype men in the same manner as men stereotype women. He brought life into my life. We have a grown family and, though

I am retired, I still lecture occasionally. I'm happy, although like everyone, I sometimes wonder what could have been."

"What about us? It seemed more than just escape."

"Of course it was," she said. Our relationship was like Latin. Although it is a dead language, it is not extinct. It doesn't grow or shrink by adding and dropping words like a living language . . . but it has functionality. Our love was like that. It was useful but it could not grow."

I took a small notebook from my pocket, wrote *si vis amari ama* in it, and handed it to her. "Do you think we should finish our experiment with *veni, vidi, vici?*"

She made a face like she had just tasted old fish, took my hand, and introduced me to her husband who had been sitting in the audience. He seemed a decent man and it occurred to me that she had indeed found her life while, in a way, I was still searching for mine.

❧

Adriana smirked. "So sex with you is like reading a book. I'd wager that she was thinking of short fiction. But seriously, have you considered that, often when we search for something, it's nearby, unnoticed as we stare into the past at something we thought we had?"

I missed the import of her words and she continued. "You said that at times you felt as if you didn't exist. Maybe it was a lack of self-esteem. You were ignored and as your infatuation limited the size of your world, you didn't exist in that world."

"I understand that, but what about Philomena?"

"Philomena was living an unnatural existence, trying to conform to the standards that society, Don Rodolfo, and her family had set for her — she valued herself according to the degree of their acceptance. She knew of no other standards.

Her attempt to escape through you caused guilt and confusion, because daily she was thrust back into a restricting environment. You were her deliverance but you were also the instrument of her guilt and that conflict made the world seem unnatural — a place with no space for her, hence a place where she could not live."

I left Adriana's in a sober mood and walked home beneath a silver moon. What she had said made sense. The search for love is the pursuit of something missing in ourselves — a desire to slip away from our own company and mesh with another. Finding it produces ecstasy, rapture, and intoxication — not unlike those other hazardous antidotes to aloneness — alcohol, drugs, and religion.

I had not recognized my relationship with Philomena for what it was and I felt regret, not for my lack of understanding — at the time I was young — but regret that the barriers that surround us are so opaque that they cloud our vision of what might be.

Lilacs Have That Effect

MY FATHER'S WEALTH HAD BEEN ACQUIRED when he was young so his portrait of life had a more elegant frame than my mother's picture of the world. She came from an area of town known as Hump and Dump Alley. It is from her that I acquired my passion for the earthy side of life, although this was an aspect of her nature that she kept secret from my father, a stern patrician who never smiled. He believed that having sex for enjoyment made as much sense as breathing air for its nutritional value or sleeping in order to lose weight. He was fond of saying that everything should be done for a purpose and pleasure did not qualify. His main interest in life was finding shortcuts and he banked time the way a squirrel hoards nuts. He kept his hair short and wore a beard to save the few minutes each day it would take to comb and shave. Every evening he arranged his clothes along the hallway so that in the morning he could dress en route from his bed to the bathroom — and, once in the bathroom, he used a stopwatch to time every activity from brushing his teeth to emptying his bladder.

I never understood how my mother and father tolerated one another but somehow their marriage succeeded. It has been my lifelong fancy that more than serendipity was responsible for my creation — a magical waltz perhaps, a beautiful sunset, or even a romantic poem. Both died carrying their secret, however, and I'm afraid I shall never know.

Of course Adriana has speculated. "You must be adopted," she said. "It would be impossible for your mother's good looks and your father's intelligence to combine and produce someone like you, with a face that would frighten a statue and an IQ that is less than the temperature on a cold day . . . and speaking of IQ, how did someone with your obvious limitations gain entrance to a university? Did you bribe the registrar?"

"No, I didn't . . . but you have accidentally sailed close to one of my secret islands."

"What island? Tell me," she said.

"Very well, but only in the interest of full disclosure. I don't need a lecture on the rights and wrongs of my past."

"I make no promises. Tell me."

"I said I wrote the entrance exams for university. I didn't say I gained acceptance."

"I know you attended. How did you get in?"

"About the same time that the university failed to recognize my academic potential, my parents ended their lives the same way that they met, in an automobile accident. The sadness came with a silver lining: the key that unlocked the front door to higher education, but only after the university set out the welcome mat."

"I don't understand."

"I arranged an appointment with the president of the university, told him the sad news and that in Mother's and Father's memory, I intended to heavily endow the institution that I attended. I further explained that I had been considering both Harvard and Oxford but that I harboured a secret soft spot for his academy as it was located in my home country. I was enrolled that very day."

Adriana raised her eyebrows. "How much did that cost?"

"Nothing, my academic airhead, not even tuition. When the president enquired why my cheque was not forthcoming, I explained that it would be unseemly for me to endow while I was still a student and they would have to wait until I received my degree."

"I imagine you graduated *Some Come Loud.*"

"No, you'll be surprised to learn that marriage cut short my academic career."

Adriana kicked off her sandals. "This I must hear," she said.

I was nearing my third decade when I made the mistake that all would-be lovers make. I decided matrimony was an appropriate course of action. The success of my parents' marriage had left its mark and as I had not yet realized that I was destined to be a lover to the world in general, I was predisposed to the idea of a permanent relationship.

Her name was Elena and I first saw her in my Histrionics for Introverts class. She was exquisitely packaged and I, in the manner of a child on Christmas morning, couldn't wait to unwrap the parcel. Like a teenage fool I became enamoured by large breasts, pouting mouth, and shapely legs.

She had a way of tossing her hair and thrusting her chest at the horizon that gave the illusion she was walking uphill. Her thighs, pushing purposefully against a tight skirt, caused her hips to rock so that, viewed from behind, it was possible to see cheek jiggle with every step. She wore no brassiere and the sight of her chasing a pair of perpetually alert nipples across campus never failed to attract fawning admirers. Her perfume smelled like spring lilacs and I came to associate this fragrance with her appearance to the extent that whenever I passed a lilac bush I immediately developed an erection.

She was the embodiment of every star in all the damp nocturnal movies I had ever dreamed. I became convinced that love was just another term for the pleasant sensation that occurred near my groin whenever she passed by . . . and then I took the incredible leap of assuming that because I loved her, it followed that she loved me. Little did I know that this was the same twisted reasoning used by all who talk about love at first sight.

❧

Adriana set my thinking on a straight road. "Calling you a halfwit is two times generous. Your body doesn't contain enough blood to operate your brain and your penis at the same time. Do you know how ludicrous it is to believe that having an itch will cause someone else to scratch? Do you also expect free meals when you are hungry, or complimentary brandy when you thirst?"

"But I was in a daze," I protested. "I felt like I had been dead my entire life. Falling in love shattered that illusion, but I knew that I could not be truly alive until Elena acknowledged her love for me. It was a very intense time."

"You are simple," she said. "Usually a lover's degree of passion is related to the extent of prior loneliness. As the term 'being in heat' applies only to animals, your obsession was most likely related to your level of lunacy."

❧

Unfortunately Elena chose to hide her feelings for me, pretending that she wasn't impressed by my urbane wit and sophisticated manner. Her act was good — so good that she daily forgot my name, though I shouted it out whenever we met.

Inspired by suppressed desire, I became aggressive in my attempts to gain her attention. I took to standing on the steps of the library in order to speak to her as she passed by on her way to class. She steadfastly ignored my cheery, "Good morning." When I held open the door to her classroom, she swept by with her nose in the air. After a few weeks I decided to increase my visibility. The autumn days had become cool and as the trees and shrubs took on the drab colours of fall, I did the opposite. Hoping to jar Elena into acknowledging my existence, I began to vary my attire, progressing from green suits with yellow ties to long red underwear with top hat and tails. She didn't notice.

One chilly morning I removed all my clothing except for a pair of red polka-dotted boxers. I might as well have been a bad copy of a Greek statue. Finally, bursting with suppressed hormones, and rationality blocked by desperation, I stood on my head wearing only my yellow tie. I was arrested for public indecency but I couldn't have been happier. The ice had cracked! She was in stitches as the police wrapped a blanket around me and threw me into the patrol wagon. Days later, when I returned to campus, she smiled at me although she still didn't speak.

It was her attitude that made me determined to dive head first into the pool of committed men. I didn't see how we could fail. Between us we possessed the only two requirements I considered necessary for a successful relationship — she was attractive and I was rich. Expense was unimportant. If that's what it would take then I was prepared. From flowers to costly jewellery I smothered her with every type of affection money can buy.

Cash worked where all else had failed and we began dating. She explained her previous aloofness. "You excited me so much I didn't think I could control myself," she said. "Fortunately my religious upbringing taught me to suppress desire. I can turn away from intimacy even when I'm smouldering inside."

She discouraged other suitors by pretending indelicacy — chewing gum, swearing, and referring to the act of love as "a trip to the bank." My roommate, Edgar Martinez, wasn't impressed. "She's frigid," he said. "When she spreads her knees everyone in town puts on a sweater."

My libido was in constant turmoil and as I spent more time with her the ache in my groin turned to rigid obsession. She had a habit of letting her skirt ride up which caused me to become practically incoherent as my entire brain strained itself in a futile attempt to focus my eyes on the shadows far up her thighs. Once in a crowded café she slipped her shoe off, smiled coyly and explained that a diamond ring was the best aphrodisiac ever invented, while beneath the table she massaged my personal accoutrements with her nylon-covered toes.

Once, late at night, I parked my car on Foreplay Ridge and we kissed. She allowed small liberties as her tongue probed deep into my mouth. After an hour my scrotum swelled to resemble a blue soccer ball and I was barely able to whimper goodnight before speeding home to find welcome solo relief.

She explained that she was letting our passion build for a special night when there would be an explosion unlike any since hot lava burst from Krakatoa's smouldering crater to spill over an innocent landscape. I came to understand that the special night would be our wedding night and I began to imagine matrimony which I thought I could float into with impunity. Oh foolish me! I now know that no man who makes that trip ever returns to where he started. It's like believing that flatulence and moveable arms will propel one through water like a porpoise, which is a safe enough delusion so long as one doesn't plunge into the deep end of the pool. But plunge I did. We were wed exactly six months after I first set eyes on her.

The day of our nuptials was cool and beautiful. The mountains that ring Lake Albatross provided a postcard-like backdrop to our ancient university buildings, and the sun created purple shadows on the slopes where elongated sepia strips delineated wet season run-off valleys. Wisps of cloud dangled over the peaks and encircled the summit of Mount Albatross like a wedding band circles the finger of a virgin bride.

Elena had decided that we could not be married in the campus chapel because it was too small to accommodate all of her relatives and the several hundred other guests that she had invited. The ceremony was held off-campus in the Church of Our Lady of Perpetual Devotion, presided over by Father Alvarez, an elderly priest who came late to his calling after working many years as an interior decorator. In the dim afterglow of two successful careers, the good father spent much of his time reliving his past. Because of his habit of continually rearranging candles, banners, lamps and art, including statues of the saints and the Madonna, the church had become known to local parishioners as Our Lady of Perpetual Motion. I was unaware that the result of this particular ecclesiastical transaction would be an almost permanent attachment to my own Lady of Perpetual Indulgence.

Elena's sisters, Pantagruel and Gargantua known affectionately within the family as Panty and Gargle, served as bridesmaids, and her uncle gave her away. Because I had few relatives and no close friends, Elena's brother, Nacho did me the honour of standing as my best man.

Everything proceeded as planned. Father Alvarez pronounced us man and wife and beamed as I placed the ring on Elena's finger — a ring that she had picked out and which weighed as much as a small tractor. He said I could kiss the bride but when

I raised her veil she giggled and turned away so I only tasted the perfume of her ear. It was lilac and it produced the usual reaction. A small tent formed in my trousers and led the way as we proceeded up the aisle toward the rear of the church.

Our reception was held in the Casa de Cultura which was festooned with flowers and crepe. Elena had helped with the decorating and it was obvious that a number of local florists would soon be driving larger cars. She had hired the city's finest dance band and the value of the food and liquor on display rivalled the financial reserves of a small country.

There were many speeches by Elena's relatives. Nacho's toast to the bride was joyous. "This is the fourth marital project that Elena has attempted, yet she has never suckled the warm milk of success," he said. "But this time she has latched on to a full breast and we, her family, are eagerly looking forward to our turn at the nipple." I found it puzzling that this statement produced a loud cheer and I received so many slaps on the back I was sore for a week.

❧

Adriana, fortified by brandy, couldn't stop crowing. "You had too many pesos for your brains, old man. She almost sucked you dry. You would have saved a lot of money were it possible to hire wet-nurses to replace idiots."

❧

Our nuptials were celebrated deep into the evening. Eventually most of the guests demonstrated their unfamiliarity with free liquor by passing out. The exception was Elena's mother. Holding her glass against my left ear she steered me around the dance floor, pausing only when her drink needed to be replenished. As the evening progressed she became unsteady and gripped me tightly for support. She was not a small woman and it was all I could do to keep her from sliding to the floor. Occasionally she gained control of her balance, straightened, breathed into my face and repeated the same phrase. "My little girl has a delicate personality. I'm concerned that you won't treat her right so I've decided to live with you." Like a naïve fool I assumed it was the liquor talking.

✿

Adriana's response was to cackle. "I think you should have married the mother," she said. "You might have become a better dancer."

✿

Eventually it was time to embark on our honeymoon. We left the reception in a taxi and caught the late ferry to Isla del Amor, the island of love. The night was perfect. A large yellow moon hung over an inky ocean and music drifted along the beach chased by wisps of oleander and cinnamon bush. Waves caressed the warm sand and their rippling sound followed a path of moonlight to the open window of our suite at the Rose Posada.

I ordered oysters and champagne, quietly so as not to startle Elena — she was in the bathroom preparing herself. Then I removed my clothes, applied cologne, and donned my honeymoon ensemble. My fantasy was about to come true — no, a lifetime of fantasies was about to come true. My order arrived and I poured two glasses of champagne.

"What's all this?" Elena asked when she emerged from the bathroom. My glow-in-the-dark bikini shorts were only partly covered by my gold satin bathrobe.

"A prelude to the wonders to come . . . but why are you dressed like that?" I asked offering her one of the glasses. She was wearing blue jeans and a sweatshirt.

She ignored my question. "Order more drinks," she said. "Gargle and Mama are joining us. They have nowhere to stay so they'll be spending the night here. I've found you a room down the hall." She guzzled the champagne and tossed the glass out the window. I heard it smash on the patio tile.

So there it was — my honeymoon fantasies dashed and broken like Elena's champagne glass. I spent the night on a narrow cot in what must have normally served as a storage closet for brooms, mops, and maid's supplies. Even my imagination proved to be poor company. I was so upset that I ended the evening beating my head rhythmically against the closet door.

Elena's family immediately moved into my house and I was generally ignored, except for those times when I took on the identity and function of a bank teller. Unfortunately, my wife was not blessed with anything like my accommodating personality, and her disposition effectively ruled out the expression of either my feelings or my fluids. Starting on our wedding night and continuing through our marriage, she not only refused to sleep with me but rather took a keen delight in deriding my personality, my physique, and my manhood. She said that I should have become a priest because given my lack of libidinous attributes the vow of celibacy would have been easier for me than that of silence for a deaf mute.

For the most part her family echoed Elena's sentiments. Her sister, Gargle, was the exception. She made no secret that she would be happy to come to my bed, but contrary to the implication inherent in her nickname, she was possessed of such an acute case of halitosis that wallpaper voluntarily disengaged itself whenever she walked down a hallway. I politely ignored her invitations.

I will not bore you with the tale of my confinement in Elena's connubial prison. Suffice it to say that the term I served while shackled by the bonds of matrimony was all hard time with no respite for good behaviour. I became a model prisoner, however, and was eventually able to effect a release by severing myself from a generous portion of my inheritance.

❧

I had not seen Elena for over fifty years. My search for her proved difficult but she had not left the city and eventually I tracked her down. She and Gargle were sharing a small room in a church-sponsored home for retired women of elastic virtue. Her residency at the home was not voluntary. She had replaced her lack of passion with a love of food and had grown exceedingly large — so large that she was no longer able to function in her chosen profession. She was now unemployed and penniless after a long service as an officer in the war against moral rectitude. She had descended through the ranks from high-priced call girl to working in a common bawdy house, eventually ending her career in the streets competing with a cohort of 'peso pussies', grimly plying a trade for which she had no liking or talent.

"Why?" I asked. "You separated me from enough money to last three lifetimes. What happened?"

"Oh," she said. "I developed a love for the gaming table as well as for food. My family also acquired an incomparable ability to spend. The money did not last long."

She exhibited no sentiment and though I had expected to feel rancour, I could not be bitter after I saw her circumstance. Our meeting failed to generate any emotion. Instead I felt the same bleak nibble of frustration experienced by someone who selects a winning horse but discovers the odds are such that only the wager is returned at the betting window.

As I stood to escape, I detected a familiar scent. Elena still wore lilac perfume. The familiar fragrance caused an unfamiliar stirring and I turned toward Gargle in search of an antidote. Her breath neutralized the lilac. I left and returned home to face Adriana's curiosity.

"Did you retrieve any of your lost vanity?" she asked. "Did your meeting trigger fears of conjugal bliss? Is there a lasting lesson when avarice meets pretentiousness?"

I pondered Adriana's questions. Elena had desired neither an intimate relationship nor a home. Her sole objective in leading a willing me to the altar was to lighten my unbearable load of financial viability which she saw as preventing me from living a pure and uncontaminated life of penury.

The distance from love to where no trace lingers is five times longer than the distance from first encounter to complete enchantment. What starts as shared kiss frequently turns to shared house, shared relatives, shared wallet, shared bank account, and shared malaise. As the Buddhist says, there is no permanence in this world. Perhaps it's fated that the one you adore today — the core of your cosmos and passionate heartthrob — will eventually become your most odious nightmare.

Adriana, who has herself nibbled matrimonial cake on at least five occasions, is stoical. "Many of my choices were not the best quality of husband material," she said. "However, I could always overlook their shortcomings when I was fully occupied with their shortcomings. You, old man, were forced to endure the hardship of unrelieved lust while the lady derided the very desire that had allowed her to lure you in the first place. Were you not so idiotic I could possibly feel sorry for you."

I've heard that there is a little of the whore and the virgin in every woman, and that these opposites are not in conflict but are really two dimensions of the same nature. Adriana does not entirely disagree, although she adds the caveat, "The concepts are meaningless without reference to men. You are all hapless fools who try to classify everything. Elena simply played the two roles that men have been defining for centuries — two roles that serve as straight jackets to enclose other aspects of a woman's nature. I'm sure there was more to her . . . perhaps she was a female Robin Hood who took from a wealthy lackwit for the benefit of her family . . . or maybe she had an inner financial genius begging to be set free. You were deceived twice, old man — once by Elena and once by yourself. Her scheme only worked because blue balls are an affliction that spreads to the brain."

"I admit my thinking was riding a slow elevator, oh wise wart of womanhood, but that does not excuse Elena's behaviour. My conscience is spotless."

Adriana nodded. "Your problem is your inflexibility. If you had lowered your expectations as much as Elena did, then your relationship would have worked . . . and are you sure your spotless conscience isn't due to a vacant memory?"

"But she was a hypocrite," I protested. "She professed desire for me but it was my money that was the object of her yearning. If the Devil truly resides in the bowels of the earth he must spend full days directly beneath Elena's feet.

Adriana looked like someone about to drown a puppy. "You *are* wearing blinders," she said. "After all, a double-standard is better than no standard at all."

"But I was so much in love that I was a slave in the relationship." I raised my voice to overcome her laughter.

"You are thick," she said. "It wasn't love that was blind. It was you . . . and not knowing how love looks, you were fated to find it wherever you searched. You saw romance in a transaction that, at its best, contained as much warmth as the purchase of a block of ice."

"Nevertheless, Elena was my wife. Doesn't that mean anything?"

"Not necessarily. Nuptial knots may serve only to keep couples chained to the status quo while they play house. Even in a good marriage, maintaining a relationship can become a job where sex is regimented and fidelity excreted like sweat from an Egyptian slave. Elena didn't use sex to get what she wanted — only the promise of sex. You were swindled, old friend."

For a moment I thought I detected sympathy in Adriana's voice. The idea unnerved me and I left for home. Perhaps our nightly brandy was destroying her brain cells, or perhaps she was on a fast train to senility. After all, sympathy has utility only in the present. The past has no need of it. Besides, there are lessons in life that need no repetition. Either the student has died from his reckless foray into the realm of foolish experimentation or the results are so indelibly etched on his brain that no amount of suasion can induce him to repeat the venture. Love and marriage are not necessarily close relatives. I have remained single to this day.

In the Navy

THE FAILURE OF MY MARRIAGE CAUSED me to become depressed, and while many rebound from depression into the lap of another relationship I decided to seek advice as to a future direction for my life. Both my lawyer and my investment manager suggested I do this as they had become concerned by the large portion of my assets that Elena had removed from their care and hence the large portion of joy she had removed from their retirement plans. Accordingly I consulted with Colonel Humberto Escobar, a school friend of my father's and a man famous in our city for his ability to instantly penetrate the most confused circumstance, analyze all courses of action and recommend the one that leads to a desired conclusion. He had served in the cavalry and his military career had been brilliant in that he had created enough lucrative opportunities that he was able to retire to a lavish lifestyle though his army pension was modest. He now passed his days in Don Emilio's restaurant seated above the patrons in a suspended barber chair because its large cushion tempered the discomfort caused by a vigorous collection of hemorrhoids that had accumulated during the long hours he spent in the saddle. To alleviate boredom he passed out advice on problems that drifted up to him from the conversations of the customers eating at Don Emilio's tables.

As I had anticipated, his questions were penetrating. "Did the experience of marriage cause a greater wound to your ego or your wallet?" he asked.

"Each is a different affliction," I replied. "Neither is worse than the other. I expect to recover. Already my ego is impatient for me to become known in more of life's arenas . . . and the wound to my wallet is repairing itself thanks to the expert ministrations of my banker and accountant, who are both concerned for their own futures."

Colonel Escobar laughed, which caused both ends of his black handle-bar moustache to quiver like the back leg of a dog when you scratch its belly. "A man marries for one of two reasons," he said. "Either he has placed second in a match-up of intellects, or he has concluded that marriage is his only available path to sex. In either case I suggest a complete change in your existence. I suggest you join the military. There should be ample room in one of our armed forces for your ego to reassert itself and discipline should help to heal your depression. Of course there could be risk should our politicians not keep us out of war. If you find that risk too great then I suggest another occupation. Perhaps you should go to chiropractor school. Even if you have no backbone of your own you should learn to recognize one in others."

His advice was clear and I opted to join the navy. I was already a gentleman. All that was required was to become an officer. My wealth would purchase a commission and, though I expected to start near the bottom, I did not think it would be long before I reached a rank that would permit me to command, at minimum, a small fleet of destroyers.

When I told the petty officer at the recruiting office of my expectation he smiled and enquired as to my level of education. I informed him that I had left university to join the ranks of married men but that I had recently been liberated from my marriage bonds and felt that my experience on the high seas of matrimony, together with the battles I had survived, would be all the education I would require for a successful naval career. He smiled again and held out a form for me to sign.

Once he had my signature the smile left his face. "You are now a member of a long military tradition," he said. He then gave me a two hour lecture on the history of our country and the incredible role that our naval forces had played in that history. Finally, he concluded, "You leave for basic training in three days. Until then, report here every morning at 0800 hours and I'll put you to work."

"I don't think I should do that," I said.

"Why is that?" He looked surprised.

"It wouldn't be appropriate. I'm going to be an officer. Soon I'll outrank you."

The smile re-emerged. "Oh, I'm terribly sorry. I didn't understand," he said. There was something in his tone that made me suspect he wasn't quite as sorry as he said he was.

"It's minor," I said. "Everyone makes mistakes."

His smile never flickered. "Why don't you come in anyway and we'll start preparing you for your first command before you even leave for training."

"That would be decent of you," I replied.

The next morning I arrived precisely at eight o'clock but the petty officer who had invited me was not there. Instead an unshaven sailor in dungarees was sitting on a chair with his head in his hands.

"Excuse me," I said. "I joined up yesterday and I was asked to come here this morning."

He raised his head and opened one eye which consisted of a white background criss-crossed by a dozen red veins. "Wadafugyowan," he said.

I didn't recognize the foreign language he spoke so I repeated my statement. He returned his head to his hands and talked to his palms very slowly. "Get a broom and sweep the deck."

"I think you should look at me when you speak," I said. "I'll soon be an officer."

He took his hands from his face and stared at me through the red veins. "Pardon me," he said. "Let's start again. Get a broom and sweep the deck . . . asshole!"

His tone startled me and I immediately recognized that I was in the presence of a lower form of life. Instead of intelligence he appeared to be composed entirely of whiskers, suppressed violence, and loosely contained rage. For my own safety I decided to do what he said. "All right, where can I find a broom?"

He put his face back in his hands before he spoke. "It's up my ass. I hid it on you." I decided that I should find the broom on my own.

The grizzled sailor took a cruel delight in tormenting me and the next three days were not pleasant. As well, the realization dawned that I had signed up to become an ordinary seaman and not an officer . . . and there was no way out! My commitment was for three years. I wasn't sure that I could last.

I will not bore you with the details of basic training except to say that I was confined to base for four gruelling months during which time I marched, scrubbed decks, polished brass, shone shoes, cleaned toilets, and marched again.

I immediately recognized that I had little in common with my fellow recruits and I made no close friends. Therefore, on the day of our graduation, which was also the start of a seven day leave, I set out alone on a mission to unload the excruciating burden of carnal longing that had accumulated during the previous four months. Not skilled in the ways of meeting the type of woman who would readily assist in my undertaking, I had little idea of where to begin. Necessity is a willing teacher, however, so I was not worried. I determined to have a drink in a nearby bar while planning my course of action.

I entered and sat in a dark corner. Before I could order, a heavy set older lady with dyed hair and bad teeth waved at me from the far end of the room. She was wearing a low-cut blouse that exposed a goodly percentage of two of the largest breasts I have ever seen, one of which was partially disguised by an oblong brown tattoo. The three were alone and the woman beckoned me to join them. "Hello young sailor," she said. "Are you unaccompanied and would you perhaps like not to be?"

"Yes and yes," I replied. "I have this day been released from four months of endless marching and toilet scrubbing, during which I did little else but dream of the act that one performs in private with a woman of great passion and little inhibition. Perhaps you know someone who, because of necessity or desire, would be willing to help a sailor unburden himself of many months of accrued lust."

"It happens that I do," she replied. "Let me take you to her. There will be a small charge for both her time and the taxi fare."

I agreed and she then lightened my wallet of everything I had in it. The four of us crowded into the back seat of a waiting taxi. She placed her hand on my thigh and squeezed rhythmically as we drove miles into the countryside. I passed the time of the trip by trying to imagine the significance of her tattoo which resembled an overweight rugby ball. Eventually she directed the driver into a yard occupied by a dilapidated house.

"Is this where the young lady lives?" I asked.

"Yes it is," she said. "Follow me."

She opened a broken screen door and we entered a dark room where three men were seated at a table playing cards and drinking beer. As we passed, I noticed that the man with his back to me was holding three aces. They paid no attention to us and she led me to a tiny back room that I first thought was a closet. She closed the door and began to take off her clothes, exposing her gigantic mammaries. "Do you like them?" she asked. "I've named the left one Port and the right is Starboard. That way no sailor can get lost."

"What are you doing? Where is the young lady I was supposed to meet?"

"Surprise," she said. "It's me."

In ordinary circumstances I do not think that I would be capable of completing any amorous endeavour in such an environment, but after four months of confinement in quarters so close that it was impossible to find relief except on the rare occasions when I was assigned guard duty in a remote area, I found little difficulty in letting nature take its course.

Afterwards, the lady's only comment was, "My, you have a fast little thing there. If I wasn't so poor I might consider a discount."

I am a modest person and praise embarrasses me. "That's kind of you but there is no need for a discount. I have *always* been a model of efficiency. However, you can tell me what your tattoo signifies."

She looked amused and ushered me from the room. "It's a haggis," she said. "My first lover was a Scotsman."

On the way out I observed that the man was still holding three aces. Of course, the taxi had left and the walk back to the city took almost two hours.

❧

Adriana was strangely silent after I had related this portion of my story. After a few moments she spoke. "One of my husbands was in the navy," she said. "Your tale has raised memories."

The reflective and pensive side of Adriana's nature was one I hadn't seen and I attempted to jar her out of the past. "He probably joined after you married. I can understand that time at sea would be attractive to him."

She shuddered at some ancient memory and pulled herself back to the present. "Actually, he cleared the fog from my thinking. I once thought Freud was right — that I envied the male appendage. So I set out to get one. Unfortunately it came with a husband. However, because of him, I came to realize it was not the male organ I had difficulty with — it was the man attached to it. Had I met you first it would have been self-evident. But tell me, Old Sheep Gut, did your experience, brief as it was, have any effect on your development, either as a person or as a man? In your case the two are not synonymous."

"No, the incident was fleeting and so long ago I barely remember it. There is no point in trying to go back."

Adriana poured us each a brandy before she spoke. "I'm feeling nostalgic," she said. At the very least, tell me of your naval career."

"There was little career. It won't take long."

❧

The term of my enlistment had been shortened by two unlucky, unforeseen, and unfortunate incidents. One was mathematical and the other was erotical. The first occurred on a destroyer shortly after my training. We were steaming along the coast and I was assisting in the operation of a gun that was firing out to sea, targeting a barge anchored earlier for the purpose of practice. Unfortunately, despite my earlier exposure to port and starboard, I accidentally reversed the co-ordinates by 180 degrees and we began firing at the small coastal town of Rosarito. Nobody was injured although one shell detonated in the mayor's garden and completely destroyed a large patch of tomatoes. The mayor's beloved pet Chihuahua, Pépe, was in the garden when the shell exploded. Pépe lived through the blast but suffered such extreme psychological trauma that forever after he developed a severe case of diarrhea whenever he smelled salsa.

The recommendation of the court martial was that I be broken in rank but when they came to implement the punishment they discovered that I was already at the lowest rank possible so instead I was assigned to a term of physical labour working on the estate of Admiral Eduardo Torres, commander of the entire eastern fleet. This assignment led directly to the second incident.

The admiral was rarely home so it became the responsibility of his wife, Felicia, to oversee my labour. Even though she was much younger than the admiral she seemed to relish her supervisory role. She put me to work cutting grass, hoeing the garden, clipping trees, cleaning gutters, and painting the house. When the outside work was finished, I moved indoors to scrub floors, wash dishes, dust, and make beds.

After a few days, she came to see me as part of the furniture and began wearing what I assume was her normal daytime attire: high heels, panties, and bra. God had designed Felicia in such a fashion that her presence could cause a roomful of sober men to stagger like inebriated sailors as blood rushed from their brains to their genitals. Consequently, as she moved about the house my blood made so many frenzied return trips within my body that it carried off my thinking ability and deposited it in a part of my anatomy where Adriana says it resides to this day.

One morning I was scrubbing the kitchen floor when she called from the bathroom. I went to the door and replied, "Yes, Madam."

"Come in here," she said. "I need your help."

I hesitated, then averting my eyes I opened the door and stepped inside. She was taking a bath. "Over here," she ordered. "I want you to wash my back."

Keeping my eyes on the wall I attempted to do as she asked. When I hesitated she grabbed my uniform and pulled me into the tub. I felt a number of near-simultaneous sensations: soap went into my eyes, a nipple went into my ear, a tongue went into my mouth, and all restraint went down the drain.

Unfortunately I again reversed co-ordinates. I landed on my back with my head under water while she removed my clothes and engaged in all manner of activities that I would have enjoyed more had I not had to struggle to occasionally raise my nose into the air so I would not drown. When she was finished she allowed me to surface and smiled through the suds on her face. "It's fun to do it like dolphins," she said. I was still gasping for breath when she started again. This time we did it like frogs. Then we dozed and later, half-asleep, we did it like salamanders.

My routine changed after the bathroom incident. From that day I did little housework. My regimen consisted solely of being available whenever Felicia felt the need to give me a zoology lesson. We did it like woodpeckers, we did it like butterflies, and we did it like rabbits. During my time in her employ we aped the mating habits of mammals, fish, fowl, and of most of the insect species known to science.

One day I accompanied her to town to buy groceries. On the way home she detoured and parked at the top of a hill overlooking the harbour and the naval base. "The view from here is beautiful," I said.

"Yes, it is," she answered as she unzipped my trousers and lowered her head to get a different perspective. The scenery seemed to inspire her. "Let's do it like snakes," she said.

Soon we were naked and in the backseat. We were in the midst of what had become habitual when I sensed motion. Felicia had forgotten to set the handbrake, and by the time I noticed we were careening down the hill toward the base. I attempted to jump into the front seat so I could bring the car to a stop, but doing it like snakes made it difficult to disengage. The car chose that moment to leave the road, bounce over a ditch, smash through a security fence, cross the parade square, and penetrate the side of the administration building.

As the dust settled I was able to push open a door. Forgetting our clothes, Felicia and I crawled out. We were in Admiral Torres' office surrounded by a crowd of onlookers which included the Admiral and several high ranking officers. "I was fleeing from a snake," Felicia explained as someone wrapped a blanket around her.

My release from the navy was effective the same day I was let out of prison.

❧

Adriana no longer looked pensive. "Given your sense of direction, it's no wonder you never had children," she said. "Remind me not to follow you when you die. But tell me, Old Snake, did you find Felicia on your recent travels?"

"Yes, I did," I replied. "We met in her apartment near the naval base."

❧

Felicia and I had not seen each other since the accident. She had added elegance to beauty, was much bejewelled and smelled of expensive perfume. The years had been kind to her and I became light-headed when I saw her. These days, however, the dizziness is mitigated by the fact that all my fluids travel at a slow pace. Therefore, I am capable of carrying on a rational conversation even though Adriana says I operate with obsolete intellectual equipment.

"How are you?" I asked. "You look as if the years have detoured around you. In what manner do you fill your days that you have preserved your most vital assets?"

She smiled at me. "Much has changed," she said. "My husband sailed to his reward long ago and I returned to the academic studies I had abandoned to get married. I completed my doctorate and spent my life teaching at the university. I'm now retired."

"Wonderful," I said. "I had no idea you had an academic bent. What was your specialty?"

"Herpetology," she said. I am an expert in ophiology, the study of snakes."

I explained my mission to her. "I have become the world's greatest lover and it is my quest to find everyone who has been an influence in my life, particularly as it applies to the art and practice of love, so that I may understand what role that individual played in my reaching the lofty peak from where I now view humanity."

She raised her eyebrows. "*You're* the world's greatest lover?" she said.

"Yes I am, and I want to teach people what it is that causes friction between the sexes."

"Why? And what makes you think you're qualified?"

"Long ago I became disturbed by an alarming malfunction that I observed in the glue that binds men and women, each to the other. The glue doesn't stick and instead has hardened into a partition between the genders. Just as a lack of nutrition makes the body wither, so this missing capacity to bond causes a divide between male and female.

"I have waited years for some wise individual to inform the world of the true nature of the man-woman relationship but no one has come forward. Having spent the majority of my life engaged in the study of love, it seems that I alone have accumulated the expertise necessary to prevent an epidemic of loneliness and to ensure that humankind's next major conflict will not be between the sexes. Therefore, I wish to pass on what I have learned in a lifetime during which I climbed to the very apex of that category of men who call themselves lovers. By this means I hope to educate others to the possibilities inherent in romance. After all, love is the book that outsells all others — it is the story we read whenever we wish to restart our life."

"You never mentioned this when we were young."

"No, I didn't. I must confess that I did not begin my adulthood with this study in mind but the need for explanation grew as one-by-one I was exposed to love's handmaidens — foolishness, exhilaration, passion, unvarnished emptiness, crushing loneliness and the hopeless beauty of unrequited obsession. It was only after I had gained considerable experience that I discovered that the single greatest truth in the realm of romance is also the single greatest puzzle — that *most love is made without love* which is akin to donning a blindfold before entering an art gallery, or inserting ear plugs before listening to a symphony."

She clapped her hands. "I understand. You're the world's greatest lover in the same manner that Madame Tussaud was the world's greatest sculptor. You intend to gather your romantic creations, replicate them, and display them publicly like wax copies in a museum."

She did not seem to be taking me seriously but I ignored her derision. "Tell me," I said. "Why did you choose me?"

"Adultery is just a way of saying there's something more," she said. "I was with a man I had nothing in common with. Our lives were a parade of *maybe nots* and *wait and sees,* unremarkable when said, but they added up to intolerable boredom. There was a cavity in our lives and it was filled with all the words we didn't say. I wasn't particularly attracted to you but you were my antidote. It was as simple as that."

"Surely you once cared for each other. Why else would you marry?"

"Ah," she said. "Marriage — there's no venture that begins with so much optimism and which so often ends in tears. Even the restaurant business has a better success rate."

"But he must have wanted you at one time," I said.

"Oh, he did," she replied. "But why would a man chase a bus he had already caught? No one desires what he doesn't lack. It's true that a woman loses her lover when she takes him as her husband."

She looked at me closely and her eyes sparkled. "We're both ancient," she said. "But I wager we could still do it like sloths."

Adriana looked startled and then she chuckled. "You didn't take Felicia up on her offer," she said.

She was right. Felicia's comment about being ancient had unnerved me, not because I'm old, but because of what it implied about my future. I have reached the age where I no longer view death as a tragedy. The real tragedy is living long enough to run out of lovers because when you run out of lovers you run out of love, and when you run out of love you have outlived desire and with it your hopes and dreams.

My learning curve turned down and I psychologically crossed the threshold into old age when I noticed that I was no longer making plans to attend events that were well into the future. Gradually the time horizon shrank until I found myself, like a recovering alcoholic, living one-day-at-a-time. It's not that I can't think of the future. I can, but I feel that the risk of not seeing my plans come to fruition far outweighs the benefits that might accrue if they do. The exception is my birthday when I force myself to reminisce, when I take inventory of my aches and pains to try and discover what has changed from the previous year, and when I mentally create a straight line trajectory so I can determine how I will be feeling on my next birthday should I be so fortunate as to have one. My checklist includes memory loss, hemorrhoids, a tendency to repeat myself, an addiction to Viagra, arthritis, an enlarged prostate, chest pain, and a tendency to repeat myself. If I'd known the Good Lord was going to prickle the world's patience by keeping me around so long, I would have been less fastidious about the perspiration caused by physical exertion.

Apart from my physical health, I annually record the changes that have occurred in the way I conduct my life. Whereas there was a time when, for amusement, I raced cars, soared in hot air balloons, climbed mountains, and canoed in dangerous rivers, I now calm my adventurous spirit with the occasional game of checkers with Adriana. Also I have my crocheting which, by the grace of the good Lord, I will finish before I pass on. I am making the shroud in which I intend to be buried and across which I have stitched my epitaph in brilliant colours: *Gigantic in Love, Small in Misfortune.*

Adriana says the message is all wrong and should read, "Gigantic in my own head and small where it counts."

The conundrum is that as I get older and the world's expectations of me become less I find that some things are more interesting. For example, the realm of love is not as much populated by young people as I had always believed. Rather, it is the domain of age and experience. Few in the newer generations understand that as performance becomes less important, love itself becomes a joint venture rather than a proprietorship. This means that the amount of liability that each partner assumes varies with the occasion which, in most circumstances, should optimize the experience for both.

Love and sex are twins joined at the navel, the offspring of desire and passion. Together they run the cosmos. Universal, immutable and omnipotent, they affirm life and are the antithesis of dying. I think Adriana agrees although she says my birthday list is like a lost cohort of whining complaints marching through the evening air in search of sympathy, and that she will be happy to put me out of my misery any time I so desire.

Felicia's offer was made with neither love nor desire and, as such, it suggested that I had out-run my hopes and dreams, thus portending a future entirely too bleak to contemplate.

In Business

ADRIANA AND I WERE ENJOYING A post-dinner brandy in the garden at Cafe Dos Lunas after having made quick work of steak dinners. She was prattling but I called my attention back from its wanders in time to hear her congratulate Don Emilio on the quality of his cuisine.

"It's a marvelous restaurant you run, Señor. We're lucky to live nearby."

He dismissed her praise with a friendly wave and I jumped into the momentary silence. "This may surprise you, my muttering meat-loaf, but I once ran a restaurant that was Don Emilio's main rival."

"You were a restaurateur? How is that possible for someone who can't make toast without a recipe?"

"It was years ago and it's partly the reason that you must pay for our dinners."

"Please enlighten me. Considering how rarely you reach for your wallet, I thought that perhaps the sight of a bill caused temporary paralysis in both of your arms."

"Very well. You are aware that I once had ample resources to feed even you, my Rubenesque pot roast. It was while I was married that my financial circumstance began its retreat, heading downhill faster than a race car with a tailwind."

❧

When I was young I didn't really know my father, the nature of his business, or the source of his wealth. Therefore, when teachers or fellow students enquired, I would improvise.

"Papa struck it rich in the South African gold fields."

"My father's a world famous brain surgeon."

"He's a retired movie star."

The truth, I eventually discovered, was that my father had inherited some wealth but he had joined the ranks of the very rich by founding a chain of high-end eateries that were located in every major city in the Americas. I acquired them on his passing. You may remember — his name was Bernardo and the restaurants were called Bernardo's Beef Bistros. The specialty was steak, ribs, and other beef dishes. They served everything from Filet Mignon to Chateaubriand and they were Papa's pride and joy; he had built the enterprise starting with one hamburger stand on the malecon in Aguas Profundas.

When he first expanded, he had allowed his brother Alphonso to acquire a limited number of shares, which made him a minority stakeholder in the enterprise. Alphonso, in turn, had left his holdings to an assortment of kin who, until my father's demise, had been content to cash their annual dividend cheques. Unfortunately, the dividends eroded steadily during my stewardship and were in danger of being washed away completely in the wake of my divorce.

My cousin, Alphonso Dos, had always been jealous of my nimble wit, carefree banter and ability to leap over pitfalls placed in my path by either man or nature. He was a lawyer and an animal lover who used his dividend cheques to finance and run a shelter for unwanted dogs. He owned a dachshund named Piggy who he had rescued from near starvation and a life of vagrancy. Piggy had thrived and was now extremely overweight. She never left Alphonso's side and he, in turn, loved her like his own child.

When the dividends dried up and his dog shelter was threatened with closure, Alphonso called a meeting of my relatives and expressed concern at the rapidity with which my lifestyle was depleting the value of the company. The result was an application to the courts, citing my incompetence as a reason to nullify Father's will.

To combat Alphonso's legal assault and to rescue Papa's legacy, I decided that the company needed a large injection of cash. The idea of work was abhorrent to me so I determined to find an easier means of acquiring money.

The waiter brought our bill and Adriana reached for it. "I'll pay," she said. "I see where this conversation is heading. What did you do?"

"I decided to patronize the racetrack. I mean, how difficult could it be to decide which horse will arrive first out of a field of only eight or ten? I determined that most who wager at the races analyse the wrong factors. They look at things like past records and track conditions."

"What did you do, read jockey entrails?"

"Not at all. I approached handicapping very scientifically. I looked at pedigrees."

"That makes sense. Knowledge of the sire and dam should provide clues as to how the offspring will perform."

"Not the *horse*! I looked at the rider's pedigree. I reasoned that if a jockey came from the right social background and parentage, then he would be a winner . . . and he would automatically transmit that attitude to the horse.

"I then went to a major track in the United States to test my system. Unfortunately the test exposed a factor that I had not considered. Though I had handicapped the race, I had not taken my own handicap into account."

"I understand. The second coming could happen three times before you'd be able to deal with all your handicaps."

"I'm serious. It happens that I have a mild form of dyslexia which caused me to bet on the wrong horse. For example, if I went to the betting window with the intention of putting two dollars on number ten, I would inevitably bet ten dollars on number two."

It sounds like you needed to find a bookie."

"That's what I did, but my problem didn't go away. If I wanted to place 5000 on number five in the third then I found myself telling the bookie to place 5000 on number three in the fifth. Soon, I had depleted all of my resources and a great deal of money that belonged to the company."

"No wonder I have to buy dinner. You can't keep numbers straight."

"That's not all. One afternoon I was bemoaning my luck to a gentleman I met in the bar. He told me a sure-fire way to recoup everything. He was a horse owner and had succeeded in getting an unknown named Hole-In-Your-Pocket into its first race against competition that had no chance. The young filly was extremely under-matched and the odds would be astronomical. With a large bet I could get back all that I had lost. I placed a mortgage on our corporate headquarters and withdrew the company's complete line-of-credit. Then I wrote out my bet and gave it to the bookie."

"The race unfolded just like the man said. Hole-In-Your-Pocket led from the start and soon was so far ahead that there was no chance she would be caught by any horse in the field."

"Did you get rich? How much did you win?"

"No. Unfortunately I lost everything."

"How could that be?"

"In the homestretch, with less than 100 metres to go, the jockey fell off. The other nine horses finished while Hole-In-Your-Pocket trotted over and began grazing on the infield grass."

"Is that when you lost the restaurants?"

"Not yet. I still had an ace up my sleeve. I had no choice but to repair the company's ills so even though I hate work, I adopted a hands-on approach to running the restaurants. The task wasn't easy as we were in the midst of a severe recession.

"My first and most crucial goal was to dam the flow of red ink. To attract new business and increase revenues, I implemented a brilliant strategy. I reasoned that many people spend a good deal of time dressing and primping before dining out. They then arrive at a restaurant only to be told that they have to wait for a table. I thought, *why not combine the two events?* Consequently, I remodelled the entrances to all of our restaurants to include barber shops, beauty parlours, showers, and changing rooms so that a customer could arrive directly from whatever sweaty activity that he or she chose, have a haircut and set, apply makeup, shave, shower and dress for dinner while waiting for a table."

"Brilliant, you say, did you gain even one new customer?"

"A few. However, we found that many people made reservations, used our waiting area to dress, and then left to dine at other establishments. The cost of operating the new facilities actually accelerated the drain on the company."

"Sounds bad. What did you do?"

"I decided that the red ink could only be contained by brutally slashing costs. An examination of profit and loss showed that by far the biggest expense was for the high quality beef that we served.

"Unfortunately, without beef there was no business. I could see only one way out of that dilemma. It was necessary to cut out the middleman. I immediately stopped all dealings with abattoirs and began buying only cattle not destined for slaughter. For the most part these were animals that were near or already dead so they could be acquired for little or no cost. Besides, I considered slaughterhouses and abattoirs to be cruel and inhumane. What better way to stop the unethical killing than to serve meat from animals that had already lost the ability to care for themselves?

"All this produced a dramatic improvement to our bottom line so I decided not to fight with a good thing. I expanded the operation to include other inexpensive meats that were freely available on the sides of highways. We added each new delicacy onto our menu as a Chef's Surprise."

"I don't believe it. Did you get sued?"

"No, my gibbering gourmet. Business improved. We kept the source of our dinners to ourselves, reasoning that it gave us a competitive advantage. We also lowered our prices and had lineups everywhere but in a few locations where our new menu items were old hat."

"Where would that be?"

"Some places had anticipated our strategy. We found competitors in Saskatchewan, Georgia, and Montana who carried items on their menus such as Flat Frog Flambé, Prairie Dog Paté, Dead and Gone Fawn, and Stiff Donkey Stew."

"So, what did you do?"

"I thought, *Why not meet this competition head on?* We developed advertising campaigns in every country. Using a series of spots on radio we introduced each menu item with catchy ads that we thought people would remember. I'm sure you recall at least some of them. For a while they were on everyone's lips."

"Refresh my memory, meat man."

"There were many, but a few should suffice. You must remember slogans such as:

Gopher and Grits — a southern treat with tiny feet . . . or, *Supine Feline — found on Route 99.*

How about *Noodles and Poodles — Italian pasta with a French flavour . . .* and, *Fricassee of Chickadee — the best of Highway 63.*

There was also *Corgi on a Croissant — lost his bark to a fresh tread mark . . .* and, last but not least, *Roasted Toad — fresh from the road.*"

"Stop before I get sick. Did you pull it off? Did the restaurants survive?"

"Yes, they did . . . and I almost did. Alphonso dropped his lawsuit when the dividends restarted. He even took to dining in the restaurant. Occasionally, he even brought important clients. All was going well until one evening when we were very busy and started to run short of menu items. Our practice, when this happened, was to send some of the restaurant staff out foraging. Normally, they returned with ample supplies and that night was no exception. We recovered with barely a ripple and were catering to a full house when suddenly there was an incredible wrenching wail from the dining room.

"I rushed in. There was cousin Alphonso, white as a sheet, sitting with a shocked expression on his face as he contemplated a cooked and glazed Piggy, resplendent on a silver platter holding a shiny red apple in her mouth.

"Alphonso redoubled his efforts and, aided by the resulting publicity, he quickly broke father's will. He placed himself in command and then successfully sued for all of my other assets saying they had been acquired with money taken from the company. I was allowed to keep my house or I would have been left on the street with little more than I'd had on that fateful night when mother pushed me into this world. I have only one confession."

"What's that, Purveyor of Pet Pie?"

"I generally preferred dining at Don Emilio's as, frankly, the food was better."

Dear Loveworn

IT WAS THE RAINY SEASON. MY father, only ten years old, sat near an open doorway and tried to guess the position of the sun behind the elephant-grey blanket that covered the sky. Water ran over his feet below the edge of the sidewalk. He heard the squeak before he saw the small bedraggled creature and without a thought he reached out and snatched a mouse from the swirling current.

"Did you get it?" asked Ramon, aged eight, who was passing by on his way to buy corn so his mother could make tortillas.

"Yes I did. Stay and we'll catch one for you."

Fleeting, but it was the first meeting between Papa and Ramon Ortega. Years later Señor Ortega would bear the weight of my life in his hands much as my father had held the tiny mouse.

❦

Alphonso's success in court made it necessary for me to seek regular employment. I had accumulated a great deal of insight into the art of love, or rather on the difficulties that love poses, so I determined that I could be useful to both humanity and my bank book by sharing my expertise.

I was approaching the midpoint on my journey to the three score and ten that we have all been promised. Most commentators say that males reach the peak of their sexual ability at a much younger age, but just as acquiring new knowledge opens up more knowledge to acquire, I maintain that a properly informed and practiced man never reaches his peak. This claim, of course, is predicated on the expectation that a lover will continue to widen the scope of the subject by memorizing new landmarks in the dominion of passion and learning by heart every significant signpost on life's erotic highway.

I was a social person and did not relish the idea of putting in the hours of solitude required to transcribe the entire body of lore that I had accumulated. Therefore, I decided to approach Señor Ramon Ortega who was the senior editor of *El Plagio*, the largest newspaper in the country — the same Señor Ortega who, as a boy, watched my father catch the wet mouse and who became his lifelong friend. To avoid creating a book I had decided that the best way to reach a large audience was to write a regular column. To this end I constructed a sample and made an appointment. In retrospect I'm afraid that my small column was too sophisticated. I had titled it *The Odds of Love* and the señor read it out loud:

> Three aspects of any romantic association are love, friendship, and sex. Each partner brings into the alliance different expectations concerning these factors. For each individual there are fifteen possible ways the expectations can be combined, and thus for two people, there is less than a four percent chance they will see eye-to-eye. Given the myriad of other issues facing any couple, it might be safer to bet on the exact moment of a shooting star than to wager on the prospect of a successful relationship.

Take, for example, the curious case of Harriet and Salvadore, both immigrants to our nation and both lonely people. Outwardly they had much in common — each had a desire for love and friendship. However, the third factor proved problematic.

From the time of his earliest memories people had marvelled at certain of Salvadore's physical features. Situated on top of his average-sized body was an extremely tiny head matched perfectly at the other end by a pair of the smallest feet anyone in his home town of Plonsk had ever seen. The Lord had compensated, however, by being overly generous in another area. From the first "My God it's gargantuan" expleted by the midwife who delivered him, to the "It's really true" uttered in awe by the housewife who had perched in a tree outside his bedroom window, he had grown used to hearing exclamations of surprise, jealousy, lust and all other manner of emotions. The appendage that caused such outpourings grew to be Salvadore's proudest possession. Sometimes, to counter the feeling of inferiority occasioned by malicious comments about his head or feet, he would surreptitiously display his famous accoutrement. The predilection for public display would have landed other males in difficulty. In Salvadore's case, however, people came from miles around just to see if the rumours were true. His family, tired of being spied upon, encouraged him to emigrate.

Señor Ortega stopped reading, shook his head and looked at me with a sad smile on his face. "Did you really write this?" he asked.

"Of course I did. I don't know any ghostwriters."

"Perhaps you should find one," he said. "I knew your father for years. He caused me to forget my mother's tortillas. Are you sure you're not adopted?"

"I don't know why people always ask me that," I said but the señor had again started to read:

Harriet came to this country because she had over-imbibed vino at her close friend's wedding — over-imbibed to the extent that she had carelessly unlatched the gate on her moral fence. It swung open and the groom's best man tip-toed through, and then he wandered into her uncharted territory. The journey happened at the reception as they giggled together under the banquet table where they had crawled to tie Father Daniel's shoes together. She preserved no memory of the event and thus, when she found herself pregnant, Harriet surmised that God had chosen her for the next virgin birth. Father Daniel, fully recovered from a bad fall he had sustained just after the wedding banquet, assured her that this was unlikely and that her condition probably had more to do with the Devil than with God. Her mother, who had fainted at the news, took Harriet aside and added her own morsel of wisdom. "Every man has some of the Devil in him," she said, "and the size of a man's organ is a barometer which measures the extent that the Devil has gained possession of his soul. The bigger he is the more Satan has a foothold. Remember forever, the smaller the better." Both her mother and Father Daniel encouraged Harriet to move away to have her baby. The groom's best man, who was married, decided that discretion was an attractive characteristic and chose to remain silent.

Harriet met Salvadore a few years later when she stopped her Volkswagen to rescue him. He was being pursued by a few overheated matrons intent on a second look after he had carelessly dropped his bathing trunks at a local beach. He jumped into her car and the attraction was instant. Harriet, brimming with loneliness, had much to give. Salvadore, always an object of curiosity, was starved for affection. They became friends. Then they fell in love and soon they were making wedding plans.

Harriet had not forgotten her mother's words, so on their wedding night when Salvadore revealed the enormity of his desire she knew that it was not God's generosity that was involved. It was clear that the Devil had staked out his territory, and a very large territory it was, too. Salvadore, oblivious to her consternation, assumed that she was as amazed and proud as he, and he whispered in her ear that she was a very lucky girl, indeed. Harriet donned a bathrobe, left the hotel, and walked to the nearest church where she took refuge until the marriage could be annulled.

In any romance there is both a giver of love and a recipient. Unfortunately, these two look at their relationship from distinct angles. Just as two people standing back-to-back on the top of a mountain have differing views of the world, so too will a couple poised on the crest of love experience disparate vistas. The perspective of the lover is never the same as that of the beloved for it is not possible for one individual at the same time to act as both purveyor and object of love. Therefore, as with Harriet and Salvadore, expectations will always differ.

Señor Ortega put down my manuscript. "Do you think you could keep this drivel up for fifty-two weeks a year?" he asked. "I can't allow tripe in my publication. We would lose our readership. The illiterate do not buy newspapers. And your statistics . . . they remind me of an old lunatic I heard of years ago who wrote an entire medical text based on the fact that each human has on average one breast and one testicle."

He then contorted his face as if he had just discovered a dead mouse on his doorstep and said, "Out of respect for your father and against my better judgement, I'm going to hire you. My advice columnist, Señorita Gloria Amorio has just quit and moved on to work for a prominent politician. Her job is available if you want it."

"What did she do?" I asked.

"She dispensed counsel to readers who sent in problems." She did this by doing research and interviewing experts. She then wrote a succinct reply to each letter. We publish a selection of the letters and replies in every edition of the paper. It is similar to what you are proposing as many of the letters deal with problems encountered in the various stages of a relationship. Taken together they constitute a primer on how to bewitch, hitch, bitch, and ditch. We call the column *Amorio en amor* although around the office it is popularly known as The Bellyachers Guide to Boffing."

When I related all this to Adriana she said, "You mean you were hired *after* he read *that?*" She shook her head, not unlike the way Señor Ortega had all those years ago. "Did you take the job? What became of Salvadore and his gigantic friend?"

"If you'll bear with me, I'll tell you."

But Adriana's train of thought rarely stops for a crossing. "I know all men aren't created equal," she said. "I discovered that God wasn't fair when I met you. If He truly did compensate for a person's shortcomings, you would wear the largest hat in the country."

"No one has ever complained, my little glue pot," I said.

"Maybe they were left speechless by the sheer disappointment after a large expectation," she chortled.

❧

Not being the type of man to throw his last dollar into the pot when the game is lost, I accepted Señor Ortega's offer. I soon discovered that the letters submitted for my advice ranged from the mundane to the erotic and covered subjects as widely disparate as animal husbandry, political associations and the location of the most sensual spot on a lover's anatomy. I also determined that research was unnecessary as my life experience covered such a wide range of territory that I needed no further study in the areas where questions were posed. For the same reason I had no need to consult experts.

My column became popular. I was soon receiving queries from abroad in addition to the ones flooding in from every corner of the country. I will not bore you with too great a selection as many of you no doubt recall reading them when they appeared in *El Plagio*. However, I have chosen a few that demonstrate my wide knowledge and illustrate my unique ability to rescue travelers stranded by all sorts of life's predicaments. The paper gave me the name Loveworn:

DEAR LOVEWORN: I am an eighty-two-year-old widower. I suffer from haemorrhoids, arthritis, flatulence, diabetes, heart disease, dizzy spells, halitosis, high blood pressure, and incontinence. My problem is that my hair is thinning. Do you think it's a sign of something serious? HAIR TODAY

DEAR HAIR: Yes I do. Thin hair will definitely reduce your sex appeal.

❧

DEAR LOVEWORN: I confessed to Father Gregory that I indulge in what he calls *the solitary vice*. He said it was the most destructive pastime ever practiced by sinful man and precipitates warts, blindness, impotence, sterility, heart disease, deafness, and cancer. I'm twenty-eight and according to Father Gregory I should be dead by now. Is he pulling a fast one?
SOLITARY SAM

DEAR SOLITARY: No. I think you are the one doing the pulling. You should know that self-abuse is precipitated by eating the wrong foods. Candies, cloves, peppermints, tea and coffee have sent thousands to eternal damnation. However, research has now shown that peppermint is okay.

❧

DEAR LOVEWORN: My husband, Alex, asked me to buy some sexy underwear. I thought it would spice up our marriage so I did. When I went to put it on, I couldn't because Alex was wearing it. This caused a big fight which only ended when we agreed to take turns wearing the underwear. Everything is great when I have it on, but when it's Alex's turn all he wants to do is look at himself in the mirror. Any suggestions?
TAKING TURNS

DEAR TURNS: You only have a problem if you hear the mirror tell Alex that he is the fairest one of all.

❦

DEAR LOVEWORN: Last Friday was my husband's birthday. After work a bunch of the guys took him out for drinks. He was feeling no pain by the time he came home so he stopped on the doorstep of our house, exposed himself, and tied a pink ribbon around his you-know-what. Then he rang the doorbell expecting me to answer. Unfortunately, I had arranged a surprise birthday party. All of our friends and neighbours were inside waiting to shout, "Happy Birthday." They were the ones who were surprised. He's done stuff like this before, Loveworn. Do you think I should leave him?
SURPRISED

DEAR SURPRISED: No, I don't. A boy wearing pink isn't that much of a faux pas.

❦

DEAR LOVEWORN: How big is an average penis?
SHORTY

DEAR SHORTY: The size of a penis depends on its global positioning, the phase of the moon, and a multiplicity of metaphysical factors. For example, during January in Saskatchewan the penis becomes completely dimensionless. Similarly, its magnitude has been known to go missing around the time of one's second anniversary.

❦

DEAR LOVEWORN: I'm a male student in my first year at university. In my program I'm forced to take a classics course which I don't think is relevant. Can you tell me why I have to know about old Greek guys like Pericles or Sophocles when my main interest is athletics? PERPLEXED

DEAR PERPLEXED: The ancient Greeks have much to say to people in today's world. For example, Pericles was a famous statesman who pioneered democracy for ordinary citizens. Sophocles wrote incredible plays. Themistocles was a brilliant military man. If you are not interested in politics, literature or the military perhaps you may find inspiration in the life of another famous Athenian, the great Greek athletic supporter, Testicles.

❧

DEAR LOVEWORN: What is a *ménage* à *trois?* CURIOUS

DEAR CURIOUS: *Ménage* à *trois* is a French phrase used in the science of climatology. It means *when hell freezes over.*

❧

We were sitting on my patio. Adriana scooped salsa onto a taco chip and said, "It's unfortunate the paper didn't call you Loveworm. The image would have been accurate." She cackled and reached for another chip. "Thank God no one would be silly enough to take your advice. How long was it before Señor Ortega lost his patience?"

❧

She had accidentally driven down my hidden street. One morning, after I had been working for a few months, Señor Ortega visited my desk carrying a newspaper clipping. He got right to the point. "We're being sued," he said. "Did you really advise Cecilia X. to hack off her boyfriend's penis?"

"No, I didn't. There must be some misunderstanding."

"She says you did. What was her query?"

I looked in my files. "She wrote that she was in a brand new relationship and that she had just discovered that her boyfriend liked to sit next to old ladies in church and expose himself during the sermon. She asked me what she should do."

"What did you tell her?"

"I told her to end the relationship."

"No, you didn't," he said. "I have your reply here." He read from the clipping. "Dear Cecilia: When something in a relationship is inappropriate, you must cut it off."

"I meant the relationship," I said.

"So do I," he replied. "Consider *ours* severed."

Adriana choked on her taco chip. "Most people use their brains to survive. It's easy to see that you have a death wish. Was that the end of your newspaper career, or did you continue to ride on the coattails of your father's friendships?"

"No, my tender taco, I never wrote another column. The paper lost the lawsuit but Señor Ortega forgave me. In fact, he promised to help me find other employment."

"What do you mean, *other employment?*"

"He said to contact him if I ever needed a job in the future and he would be happy to recommend me, but only as a taste tester in a cyanide factory."

"You deserved that," she said.

"I disagree. What did I do wrong?"

"Yours was the sin of omission. You neglected to educate and enlighten. There are many ridiculous myths about sex and intimate relationships that are held by otherwise rational people. You let them down.

"In the last century physicians believed that excessive chastity could be harmful to men because it was thought that stored semen turned to poison. Did you know that at one time religious law decreed sex to be illegal on Sundays, Wednesdays and Fridays, that departure from the missionary position carried the penalty of seven years penance, that uncovered piano legs were considered shameful eroticism, and the one that really irritates, that the word hysterical is derived from the Greek word for womb, hence the word hysterectomy?

"The old mythologies have been replaced by modern ones — masturbation and homosexuality are considered wrong in many religions for no logical reason. Likewise, so is birth control. Admit it. You had an opportunity to enlighten and you wasted it."

She was right, of course. Through all these years I have carried the awareness that I did not use my time productively and many of my answers were too simple. I fully realized that a husband wearing pink in public could cause deep rooted psychological trauma.

Bingo

AT THE TIME OF HIS DEATH, Gandhi owned few worldly goods: a pair of glasses, a bowl, a spoon, and sandals. Unlike Gandhi, I am much too fond of comfort to throw away the few material possessions I have left. Instead, I have made it my life's mission to unburden myself of many of the inhibitions that one accumulates simply by living in this world. I have done this hoping it will help in resolving the paradox one encounters with the realization that sex is simultaneously necessary and sinful, two attributes that can combine to put even the most mentally aware individual into a quagmire of guilt and indecision. Adriana scoffs: she says that removing inhibitions resolves internal conflict in the same manner that cutting a power line removes the requirement to stop at a red light.

Because my academic, military, business, and literary careers had all been cut short, as had my marriage, I was left with no purpose. I marched in one spot paralysed by the notion that I was destined to perform the same role for the world as pornography does for a eunuch.

The despondency did not last long. Deep inside I knew that, no matter how overcast the horizon, it was impossible for someone with my intellectual attributes to be simply another raindrop in the drizzle of human mediocrity. My natural joy of living and my indestructible good nature prevailed and I quickly recovered most of my sparkling personality. Nevertheless, like a prospector who constantly stakes sterile claims, I developed a veneer of fatalism that I used to disguise my naturally ebullient nature. I took this stance because I came to doubt the possibility of love. It seemed a fiction, perhaps created by those who, like me, had failed the attempt to grasp the brass ring on the marriage carousel.

The abrasions on my ego did not heal as easily as those on my spirit, and so one evening I went to the Café Dos Lunas to put salve on the wounds by indulging in one of Don Emilio's famous dinners. I chose a table in a quiet corner where I could be alone to ponder the vagaries of human relationships. I decided a pre-dinner brandy would be the perfect lubricant to mitigate the friction remaining in my soul. I was savouring the first biting taste, imagining the joy it would bring to hold my ex-wife's hand to the flame of the candle burning in the centre of the table, when someone behind me said, "Pardon me. Are you dining alone?"

The voice soared and dipped like a tinkling music box and it penetrated my sombre mood the way thrown pebbles perforate the surface of a pond. I turned and there she was: dark hair in ringlets, an oval face with a complexion the colour of roasted pecans, and black eyes that reflected the candle flame — eyes so hypnotic I couldn't turn away.

I summoned my wits. "Yes I am. Would you care to join me?"

She smiled. "It's easier for *you* to join *me*."

I hastened to her table and introduced myself, my negative feelings vanishing like smoke from the candle. She held out her hand. "My name is Rosella," she said. "But I've been called many things since my accident."

I noticed that she sat in a wheelchair. "What happened?" I asked.

"An unfortunate mishap," she said. "You're probably not interested."

"*Au contraire*," I answered. Sometimes, when I anticipate an amorous encounter, French expressions come unbidden to my lips.

"Very well, I'll tell you, but you must promise not to castigate me."

"I promise," I said.

She sighed. "It all started when my church held a bingo to raise funds to buy our priest, Father Sebastian, a bus ticket to San Ignacio so that he could visit his ailing sister, Bettina, who was feeling poorly as a result of being constipated for thirty-two days without relief."

"Go on," I said. "Did he make the trip?"

"Oh, yes," she said. "The bingo was successful. We raised more than enough money for the ticket. Father Sebastian went to San Ignacio and he was a great comfort to his sister because he took along a jar of special salsa made by Señora Sanchez. The señora's salsa is famous for bringing relief to those who suffer the same affliction as Bettina. Yes, the bingo was a success. It was the incident during the bingo that affected me."

"Tell me," I said.

"Very well, but remember your promise."

"I will. What happened?"

"The final game was played for a prize coveted by everyone — a chicken donated by Señora Rodriquez — not just any chicken, but one of the señora's prize hens, which are known everywhere for laying the most, the biggest, and the tastiest eggs."

"What happened?" I asked again.

"I won! I was so excited I jumped to my feet and shouted, *Bingo*! My shout startled the chicken which had been dozing on the lap of Señora Rodriguez. It flew up and perched on the bingo board which was suspended above where I was sitting. The weight of the chicken caused the board to topple and it fell, hitting me simultaneously on my back and on my head."

"You poor thing," I said. "Did you suffer a spinal injury?"

"Yes I did. But Dr. Alvarez, who was also playing and who witnessed the entire incident, has examined me and he says the injury is temporary. I will soon be able to leave my wheelchair."

"You are lucky," I said.

"It's not just the spinal injury," she continued. "As I mentioned, the bingo board also hit my head and ever since that evening I've suffered from spontaneous orgasms. They come without warning, sometimes when I am least inclined to want one."

Suddenly her eyes rolled so the pupils were not visible and her lips drew back in the manner of a wolf defending its dinner. "Oh my God . . . Oh my God . . . I'm having one now." Then she shouted for the entire restaurant to hear, "*Bingo! Bingo! Bingo!*" Her body trembled as if she was experiencing a small earthquake. After a few moments she relaxed. "They can be intense," she said.

"It would appear so," I replied.

"The affliction is bad enough," she continued, "but it has also led to social pain. My tendency to shake and cry, 'bingo' at inconvenient times has caused many of my neighbours to believe that the Devil has gained possession of me. Others think that I have been maimed by God for a grievous sin of which they are not aware. I have become a social pariah."

"That's terrible. You mean you have no friends?"

"No I don't. Not since I attended the funeral of Señor Ramon Hernandez. The poor man collapsed and died after ingesting an entire bottle of the salsa made by Señora Sanchez. It took a toll on his heart. He never recovered after rushing to relieve himself more than seventeen times in one afternoon. It was during the service as Father Sebastian was commending the soul of Señor Hernandez to heaven that I was unable to contain myself. I jumped up from my wheelchair and shouted, *Bingo*. That by itself was bad enough, but the interruption was also lengthy as I am frequently multi-orgasmic."

My heart melted for her. "You poor thing," I said. "Your plight has touched me." And indeed it had. To have the most intense joy one can experience lead to isolation is a terrible form of social disease. Just because public orgasms are rare is not sufficient reason to shun one who is pioneering such displays.

"Have you tried medication?" I asked. "I have heard that the word orgasm is short for organ spasm. Perhaps all you need is a muscle relaxant."

"No," she replied. "Dr. Alvarez has tried everything. Nothing works, except when I am able to clear my mind. The episodes sometimes come uninvited, but often they are triggered by an idea."

"What kind of idea?"

"It embarrasses me but when I saw you I thought, *Holy Mother of Saints, I wouldn't mind if he parked his huaraches under my bed*. And like that, it happened. I've tried but I can't control my mind. I even decided to become a nun, but Father Sebastian talked me out of it. He said that until I was cured and able to train my brainchildren to wear loose underwear, I would be a distraction in the convent."

A sensation settled over me and I recognized it immediately. *Oh no*, I thought, *I'm falling in love again*. With hindsight I now recognize that the sensation was sympathy. But hindsight is just foresight with no future so I remained ignorant of my true feelings. Regardless of what I now know, by the time we had eaten Don Emilio's butterscotch-covered flan and ingested four after-dinner liqueurs a delicious longing was roosting on every nerve. I revelled in the same bloated feeling of well-being that affects all good Samaritans and in my naiveté I called it love.

Our relationship, which commenced that very evening, was difficult. Rosella yelled, "Bingo," at the most inopportune times and always became detached from what I was saying during the entire time of her ecstasy. I found this disconcerting as sometimes it seemed that the most banal words would cause her eyes to roll and spittle to appear in the corner of her mouth. At other times my most intense foreplay produced no reaction whatsoever. I occasionally tried shouting, "Bingo," myself but she did not respond and, in fact, seemed to resent my encouragement. It was demanding being constantly on standby for Rosella and I was only able to cope by developing the discipline of a Samurai warrior. Nevertheless, we continued to see each other and I became more enamoured with each passing day.

She soon moved in with me and she brought the chicken, which she had named Max. "No harm must come to Max," Rosella said. "She's not an ordinary chicken. She has the power to cause injury and ecstasy at the same time."

I did not argue although I frequently felt like turning Max into soup, particularly when she perched on my back and pecked at my buttocks while I endeavoured to devote my entire attention to Rosella's erotic needs.

Adriana choked on her mirth so that it was many minutes before she could speak. "I've had encounters that lasted until I made sounds that only dogs could hear," she said. "But I've never had anyone bellow 'Bingo' in my ear." She pounded her knee and exploded again. "So tell me old Under-the-B, did Rosella ever escape her torment?"

"You'll see, my pretty purveyor of pansophism." I found it annoying that Adriana gained enjoyment from hearing about Rosella's and my predicament.

❧

Rosella became preoccupied with the attempt to find some method of control for what appeared to be uncontrollable. As Dr. Alvarez predicted, she eventually left her wheelchair. Her back was restored and she gained true mobility. Her other problem remained as before, however, and with the increased ability to move some of her prolonged orgasms became truly frightening.

The incidents even occurred during sleep. She often progressed from warning cry to culmination without waking. In the morning she had no memory of the event.

After some months the inevitable happened. The unpredictability of life with Rosella began to chafe my equanimity as did the loss of sleep. I had never been a boy scout so I found that constantly being prepared caused more agony than the bruises that appeared on my self-image due to Rosella's occasional lack of response.

I often tiptoed out during her nocturnal episodes and walked the streets until morning, killing time and pondering the unfairness of our dilemma. However, walking to kill time makes as much sense as passing wind to get rich so I decided that I needed to do something useful during the late-night, early-morning hours.

On the street I regularly met anglers — men who gained enjoyment by testing their cleverness against the intelligence of fish. They were always in a hurry, heading off early to try their luck on Albatross Bay. I envied them their single-mindedness and so decided that I too would become a fisherman. After all, how difficult could it be to match wits with a flounder?

Without telling Rosella, I purchased a tiny wooden boat that was powered by a small motor. Every morning I cruised to the middle of the bay, cast a hook into the water, and trolled in large slow circles. For hours I enjoyed the peace and tranquility. Not once were my reveries broken by even a slight tug on my line . . . or by the shout of "Bingo."

One morning I returned home to find Rosella awake and waiting for me. She was agitated and curious. "Have you a secret lover?" she inquired.

"No," I replied. "I have purchased a boat and become a fisherman. However, due to some conspiracy that only the fish and perhaps other fishermen are party to, I have not, as of this hour, caught even the glimpse of one fish."

Rosella pursed her lips into the shape of a cat's anus. "I don't believe you," she said. "I'm going with you tomorrow. I've always been an avid angler so I'll know if you're lying."

The thought of fishing must have cleared her brain because there was no disruption to my sleep that night. Before daybreak we walked to the water, untied the boat, started the small motor, and putt-putted to the centre of the bay. I steered and Rosella, surprisingly mellow, snuggled against me as the sun rose to lighten a grey occan.

I readied two lines and handed one to Rosella as she whispered in my ear, "I'm sorry for doubting you. This is so romantic. I feel like I could . . . Oh God! Here it comes . . . it's happening." Her hands flew out tossing the line. The hook caught my shirt and bit into my shoulder. My own hook swung free and penetrated my pants to lodge perilously near my most important bedroom machinery. The boat tipped and began taking on water as Rosella's cries of, "Bingo," carried over the early morning calm. Soon we were surrounded by a half-dozen boats watching as our small motor sent us in tight circles. I attempted to extricate myself from the hooks as Rosella shouted and rocked the boat. We took on more water and began to submerge.

The hooks and lines inhibited my movement and I was dragged underwater, almost drowning before I was able to free myself and swim to the surface. A young man pulled me into one of the watching boats. Rosella surfaced and was also taken into the boat. She lay on her back coughing and choking. I bent over her. She opened her eyes, looked into mine and whispered, "Bingo," for the last time. We didn't know it then, but the near death experience had repaired Rosella's impairment.

Unfortunately the fishing trip signalled the end of our relationship. Rosella attributed her restored health and miraculous escape from drowning to divine intervention. In gratitude, she decided to devote her life to God. She told me of her decision one afternoon after we had made love in blessed silence. "Father Sebastian says I'm cured. I'll be leaving as soon as I train my brainchildren to wear loose underwear."

I looked at her with new eyes. Her ankles stood out over large feet. She had a birthmark on her left hip, a triangle of soft hair at the bottom of a rounded belly, alert nipples on sloping breasts, long fingers on short arms, and a semi-permanent tilt to her head that gave her a coquettish look. She tasted like ripe strawberries and smelled of crushed almonds. She took all that with her when she entered the convent and once again I was left to ponder the irregularity in human relationships and to bask in undeserved loneliness.

❦

Adriana poured herself a brandy. "So orgasm comes from organ spasm. Does that mean that you suffer from brainism, Old Fish Bait?" she asked. "Perhaps you need a muscle relaxant to start your thinking."

She tittered at her own joke and continued. "Your feelings for Rosella were fleeting, about as deep as your common sense." She pointed a finger at me. "Admit it, you were simply intrigued by her condition."

"No, it wasn't that. After she recovered I found that I no longer felt sorry for her and my feelings changed. I have always been hooked to the idea of love. Though it has been often scorched, my yearning inevitably percolates into my soul and binds me to a vision of what could be. It was my passion that allowed me to confuse pity for love."

"Hmm . . . I wonder. What about your boat? Did you get it back?"

"No, I didn't. To this day my boat rests on the bottom of Albatross Bay. Some craft are just not designed for multiple orgasms."

"One further question," said Adriana. "Whatever happened to the chicken? Did Rosella keep it . . . and why did she name it Max?"

"They wouldn't allow a chicken in the convent so I inherited her. After a period of time I gave Max to my friend Chang Lee, the proprietor of the only Chinese restaurant in the city. Sometime later Chang Lee invited me to his establishment so that I might try a new item on his menu. Listed along with chicken chow mein, drunken chicken, and poached chicken balls was the new dish which I ordered and found delicious — bingo chicken with salsa."

"And the chicken's name . . . Max?"

Oh yes, the name . . . Max was an abbreviation . . . short for climax."

"Did you find Rosella on your travels?" Adriana asked. "Is she still alive? Is she a nun?"

"Yes, yes, and yes," I answered. "All of the above."

❧

Finding Rosella had been easy. She was now known as Sister Rose and had taught all of her years at an elementary school run by her order. She was much older but she still carried the same beauty that had originally attracted me. She appeared downcast although she now exuded an aura of contentment that had eluded her all those years ago. Time had not been kind to her in one way. She was healthy but her short-term memory was on strike so she had been given tasks that did not bear as much responsibility as teaching children. She assists in the school library and with extra time she has authored a series of children's books based on the exploits of a super chicken named Max.

I asked what memories she had of our time together. She remembered our relationship, although initially she was reluctant to talk about it.

"It was long ago," she said, " . . . a period of my life that I would rather forget. However, I will always be grateful to you for sharing my burden. I needed you, though I knew that your interest was only sympathy. After the fishing incident there was no point in staying together. I always wanted to join the church, and once the bishop knew I was cured there was no weather bad enough to stop my boat from sailing."

"I understand," I said. "Did you ever have a relapse?"

She smiled. "No, I didn't. However, to this day I experience a faint quiver whenever I attend a bingo game."

I thanked her and prepared to take my leave but she motioned me to stay. Her eyes stared into mine. "There is something you can tell me," she said.

"Anything," I answered. "What do you want to know?"

"The chicken," she said. "I hope she was treated well during her remaining years."

"You can be assured on that score," I said. "Max lived a full and productive life. Even in death she fulfilled her destiny with dignity . . . and good taste."

She smiled and her face lit up. *She's still beautiful,* I thought. *There's no harm in trying.* Aloud I asked, "Do your brainchildren always wear loose underwear these days?"

Her eyes turned toward the window. "I don't remember," she said.

I left Rosella at that point. She was a melancholy figure who had been buffeted by circumstance. Much of her life had been fraught by one random episode after another not unlike the way squares fill up on a bingo card.

Adriana scowled at me and I quickly swallowed my brandy. "Terrible," she said. "Imagine the church calling the absence of orgasm *a cure* — if Rosella were a man they would have called it a tragedy. Everything is upside down. Women have an organ whose only responsibility is pleasure but they often have difficulty achieving that pleasure. Meanwhile men lug around an appendage that has conflicting job descriptions and yet they experience gratification even when they sleep. Then they have the audacity to put pressure on women to react more like them. "

I know better than to reply when Adriana is giving a sermon so I poured myself another drink and settled back for the duration.

She continued. "You have answered one question about which I had curiosity, Old Chicken Gizzard. I thought, given your lack of skill in the bedroom, that perhaps not once in your many years had you been present during the ultimate female experience. Your tale has answered that question . . . but it has raised another. When faced with a woman who has transcended old saws like equal pay or equal opportunity and who has achieved real parity — equal orgasms — what happened?"

I opened my mouth but, like all who proselytize, Adriana answers her own questions. "I'll tell you what happened," she said. "When faced with real equality the World's Greatest Lover . . . went fishing."

"Hold on," I said. But there was no room for even one ripple in Adriana's verbal stream.

"Rosella's accident forced her to dissociate intimacy from sex and thus to experience the world of passion from a male perspective. Her affliction removed the double standard that permeates most relationships, enabling her to avail herself of sexual pleasure as eagerly and as carefree as any man. However, because of societal pressure represented by her desire to join the convent, she was unable to maintain or even enjoy her freedom. You, old man, were only a bystander to a struggle that she had to lose in order to do what she wanted to do.

"Her brief fling with equal orgasms was for naught as she willingly leapt into the arms of the church — a leap which well illustrates the dilemma faced by all women who are raised surrounded by society's precepts."

I dared to interject. "But things are no longer as they used to be. Men and women are now equal."

"Matters have not changed," she said. "The only way that women could achieve true equality with men would be to count brains instead of skulls. The world gives only two choices to a woman who is so bold as to enjoy her own sexuality. She must either do it surreptitiously or in defiance of other's opinions."

The time was late. I left Adriana riding her soapbox and made my way home to bed where I pondered her assertions. As I drifted toward sleep a thought materialized: the brain is a human's best sex organ because it is also the vessel wherein resides our capacity to love. My confusion arose because there are times when each of us is partitioned by the difference between reality and our dreams. This incongruity may be our closest friend. Without it, life would move forward without us.

A Sluggish Motor

WITH ROSELLA GONE, I WAS AGAIN left to wander alone on life's landscape and to contemplate how it was that I should be so unlucky in love. It struck me that from a mathematical point of view the probabilities were such that by this stage of my existence I should have had at least one lasting relationship. As a consequence of this reasoning I decided that I should seek professional advice. Discrete enquiries led me to Professor Martina Aguilar who enjoyed a flawless reputation, not only for counselling couples who were experiencing bumps along the matrimonial turnpike, but also for providing sound advice to clients who were so unfortunate as to be romantically unattached.

I was ushered into her office by a young man who exhibited the confidence and supercilious manner implied by a slim waist, bulging muscles, and oily good looks. He sneered, used the back of his hand to wipe the juice that had dribbled from a mouthful of mango and mumbled, "Sweet Cakes will see you now."

Professor Aguilar stood and came around her desk as I entered the room. She had a method of walking that entailed tipping forward on high heels so that it was necessary for her to quickly place one foot before the other to prevent a nose dive onto the floor. Her skirt had ridden up to expose a pair of black garters clutching the tops of dark nylons and a low cut blouse revealed the main portion of a balcony large enough to stage *Romeo and Juliet*.

She grasped a corner of her desk to gain stability as she spoke to the young man. "Thank you, Raoul. I'll see you after my meeting." He turned to leave and she surreptitiously reached out and squeezed his left buttock. He flicked her hand away with a shake of his hip, leered at me through unswallowed mango, made an obscene gesture with a thumb and two forefingers, and left closing the door behind him.

"Please excuse him," the professor said. "He acts quite immature at times." She sat on the corner of the desk, causing her skirt to gain further altitude. "But you're not here to talk about Raoul. What can I do for you?"

"I need your help to untangle a dilemma," I replied. "Though I am handsome, self-assured, and intelligent, and though I am desired by all members of the opposite sex, I have for years been unlucky in my relationships. I am here to determine how to correct that situation."

"In what way are you unlucky?" she asked.

"From the time of my first awareness of the differences between male and female, every woman that I have been attracted to has wanted something from me. When they acquired what they desired, they left. During my limited years on this earth I have been used in multiple fashions: as a target for aggression; as an instrument of revenge; as a human cash dispenser; as an antidote to a boring marriage; and, most recently, as a source of sympathy.

Don't get me wrong. I have been unstinting in fulfilling my partners wishes . . . including the donation of a mountain of money to my ex-wife. However, the relationships have all been fleeting no matter how much effort I gave to them. I find this discouraging as in most cases the women involved have gone on to lead interesting lives without me."

The professor adjusted a garter. "Your tale is fascinating," she said. "Please lie on my couch and tell me the details."

I stretched out on the couch and began to relate the romantic exploits of my life. Professor Aguilar sat next to me and took notes while she absent-mindedly used her forefinger to curl and re-curl a lock of black hair that stuck out above her left ear. Once she leaned over to better hear what I was saying and the manoeuvre caused her breasts to burst into life. After a certain amount of practice I found that I could raise and lower my voice to the precise levels required to keep her chest in perpetual motion. However, it soon became necessary to close my eyes so that I could maintain my concentration.

We continued for weeks and she gradually learned the details of my life. Several times I became so relaxed under her quivering shade that my talk slowed and she was forced to poke me to rescue my train of thought. On one occasion she allowed me to drift off to sleep and I dreamed that the mountains surrounding Lake Albatross had magically come alive and were attempting to smother me. This was not an unpleasant experience and I managed to prolong the dream. However, by the time I allowed myself to come awake, Professor Aguilar had abandoned her chair and I was alone. Everything was quiet except for a rhythmical thumping sound coming from the waiting room. I called out and the thumping stopped. Raoul opened the door and peeked in. "We've had an emergency," he said. "Your session is finished for the day."

He pulled back out of sight but I caught a glimpse of him in a mirror hanging on the office wall. I wondered at the nature of an emergency that required him to deal with it dressed only in his socks.

After numerous appointments, and after relieving me of a great deal of burdensome cash, Professor Aguilar announced the results of her analysis. "First, you must know that romantic success is only part of the equation," she said. "Failure at love is not the equivalent of not loving. The problem is that the women in your life have had fully formed personalities. They knew what they wanted and how to get it. You must find someone more compatible with yourself — a woman with no ideas at all. She ought to come equipped with a fiery nature as that indicates the capacity for passion."

"But how will I find this person?"

"What I'm suggesting is not deep science. You simply search for someone who has the potential for boundless ardour but who has not yet fully developed her mental capacity. If you have difficulty return to my office and I will assist you."

The instructions were simple and my task was clear. I knew the type of woman that I had to find but the professor had given no indication of where I was to find her. Therefore, in accordance with my logical nature I made a list of the places where men and women made contact and one by one I began to frequent them. Gymnasiums, bars, dance pavilions, theatres, libraries, and concert halls — I tried them all without success before I made my way back to Professor Aguilar's office

"I have been expecting you," she said. "Are you having difficulty with your quest?"

"Yes I am. I have frequented every location where men find women but the women that I find are not the women I am seeking."

She looked at my list. "Surely you know that the ladies who patronize these establishments do so with a purpose and if they have a purpose they are not representative of the category of female that you are searching for — someone who is herself searching but who has not yet formulated what it is that she seeks, thereby eliminating the possibility that her goal has been rationally defined, and at the same time increasing the probability that she will find you interesting."

She threw my list in the garbage. "I suspect you are the kind of man who takes a fishing rod to the desert or carries a shotgun to a trout stream. Do you not know that to attract ducks a hunter sets out a decoy, to catch a fish an angler puts a worm on a hook, and when you pursue a woman you must lure her to you?"

"I don't comprehend," I said. "What does a worm on a hook have to do with finding a woman?"

"Humans do not change," she said. "The great grandchildren of individuals who fell prey to confidence men are today being duped by charlatans who practice trades of an equally dubious nature. There are words and phrases that are as attractive to the type of woman you seek as sugar water is to a hummingbird. It is an axiom that those with an ill-defined purpose are attracted by terms and situations that are themselves ill-defined and therefore imply the least mental effort."

"I think I understand. What should I do?"

"You must go where the gullible go," she said. "Read this." She reached into a desk drawer and handed me a poster.

LECTURE TONIGHT

Do you know the secrets of youth?

Do you want to stop aging and change your life?

Do you understand the mysteries of the universe?

Find the answers at Dr. Farsante's lecture.

DISCOVER HOW TO:
REBALANCE YOUR LIFE WITH TAUTOLOGICAL ARGUMENTS,
PERFORM ALLOPATHIC DIAGNOSIS AND HOMEOPATHIC
TREATMENT BY TELEPATHIC COMMUNICATION, USE
INVISIBLE FORCES TO REVERSE AGING, AND INCREASE
MENTAL STRENGTH THROUGH SOPHISTRY.

LEARN HOW, AFTER WORKING 20 YEARS AS A QUALITY
CONTROL INSPECTOR ON THE GHERKIN LINE IN A PICKLE
FACTORY, DR FARSANTE TOOK THE BITE THAT CHANGED
HIS LIFE.

"I don't understand," I said. "I have no knowledge of the topics on the poster."

"Neither does anyone else," she said. "The old fashioned snake oil salesman hasn't disappeared; he has just transformed himself — no more horse and wagon. Now it's a magazine advertisement and an office. Don't worry. This is simply a screening device to find you a partner."

"But I won't understand any of it."

She smiled again. "That's why it works," she said. "No one understands it, no one knows you don't understand it and, most important, no one will admit ignorance."

She again reached into her desk and handed me a sheet of paper. It was a list of words. I read the first few. "*Akashic records, ketheric body, psychic umbilicus, dead orgone energy.* What do they mean?" I asked.

"These are the terms that I mentioned. Memorize them and be prepared to use them."

❧

Adriana smirked. "It's appropriate that you played a phony," she said. "The professor must have known that you wouldn't have to act. Tell me, Old Snake Oil, did you follow through? Did you go to the lecture? Did anyone show up?"

"Yes I did, and the hall was packed. Dr. Farsante was compelling and he held the audience spellbound from his welcoming statement."

᱐

Good evening, ladies and gentlemen. I was forty when an aura outlined my morpho-genetic field and gave me super luminal connectedness. The infusion of this stressless scientific energy allowed me to practise toxicological and ortho-testicular medicine. I have found that combining hormones with vitamins and using an anti-aging chelational approach produces benefits to the reproductive system, including the placental subsystem. My approach, which is analogous to holistic nutrition and colonic cellulite formation, opens our irrigative capacity to protect us from free radicals. This sacred art thus allows personalized healing along with diuretic templates. As well, the reductive process detoxifies the psyche and tunes into the vibrating frequencies of divine consciousness and tantric emotional turmoil.

It is my basic premise that only colonic irrigation and multi-peroxidal therapies result in a sense of peace through control of our emotive and umbilical forces. This keeps the energy flow from spilling into our metabolic systems. Thus modalities are harnessed to remove blockages including biofeedback and ejaculation. The stimulation of our ozonal receptors is best done with metaphysical aromatherapy, ensuring our DNA as expressed in spermal nutrition is infused with entropy.

To purchase a jar of my detoxifying anti-plasmic foaming gel, and to enrol for personalized enteric meditation, see me after the lecture. Thank you.

The meeting then broke into small discussion groups and I found myself seated at a table with three ladies. We introduced ourselves. I was immediately attracted to a pretty brunette seated on my right who said her name was Prana. The other two introduced themselves as Chakra and Astra.

Prana began the discussion. "I think we should start by defining a unifying cosmic view of reality," she said.

"I agree," Chakra agreed. "But we can only do that by interpreting all biological findings on another plane. Isn't that so, Astra?"

"Absolutely," Astra said. "And if we can get to that higher plane of connectedness we should see the future." She turned to me. "Am I not right . . . Oh, I'm sorry I didn't get your name."

"My name is Alberto," I said.

The look of disappointment on her face was so palpable that I immediately retrieved Professor Aguilar's list from my pocket and consulted it under the edge of the table. Then I hastily corrected myself, "But my spiritual name is Yinyang."

"Aren't they two opposing forces?" Prana asked.

I glanced under the table. Professor Aguilar had run the two words together. "Yes they are," I agreed. "I used to be just Yin but now that I'm in perfect psychic and spiritual balance I have added the second name."

Prana smiled at me and pressed her knee against mine under the table. I noticed a look pass between Chakra and Astra.

The meeting continued with a discussion of the seven levels of the human aura and how to not only touch the edges of our energy bodies together but to fuse them by combining our emotional and tantric spheres. I was distracted during much of the conversation as at least one layer of my auric field high on my right thigh was being penetrated by Prana's left hand. She directed her energy flow toward my cosmic centre and my etheric body began to swell and take on a high level of vibration. I looked at her and she winked, unnoticed by Chakra and Astra who were in deep disagreement about the location of energy strands in our bodies. I declined to comment although at that moment Prana's hand began to rhythmically send revitalizing energy into my strand. It was all I could do to maintain psychic balance as she manipulated my external matrix. I closed my eyes and a bluish white light moved through my nebular opening and dissolved itself into a stain on my trousers.

I opened my eyes to see Prana smiling at me. She leaned over and whispered, "I sense some residual rigidity in your external matrix. Let's find a quiet place where we can merge our astral bodies."

We took our leave and made our way to her apartment where the light that outlined our auras flickered wildly until eventually my etheric body grew too fatigued to seek out her cosmic centre. Weary beyond sleep, we talked.

"I think empyrean forces have brought us together. Don't you?" she asked.

"I don't know. I have a confession," I confessed. "I have no knowledge whatsoever of the topics that have consumed most of our evening. I only attended because I was sent by my relationship counsellor, Professor Martina Aguilar."

Prana looked shocked. "Are you sure? I also was sent to the lecture by Professor Aguilar. She said I would find the man I was looking for — someone with few thoughts of his own. She has schemed and not told us the full content of her scheming."

"I concur," I said. "I feel that I have been manipulated."

Prana laughed. "We both were," she said, "and my psychic intuition tells me that you are ready to be manipulated again."

Once more we shed the confines of our bodies and thrust beyond the world of senses, until like shooting stars merge into atmosphere, we came — together as one — back to where we started, prepared to soar again.

❦

Adriana shoved herself into my story. "So you found your dream woman," she said, "someone compatible with yourself. Tell me about your relationship, oh wrinkled astral body. Did it last? Was it as fulfilling as you wished?"

Adriana has a habit of demanding more details than is allowed by the pace of my story . . . and then she sometimes pushes right into the story itself. I refused her request. At my age it's not easy to get back to the exact point where my train of thought has been derailed. "You'll find out in good time, old woman," I said.

❦

Prana and I became lovers, but I could not shake the nagging feeling that the very quality that allowed us to meet was the same quality that permitted her to fall in love with me. In other words, the aspect of her character that made her find me attractive was the same one described by Professor Aguilar — gullibility.

She said that her goals in life were simple: to find the meaning of human existence, to discover the basic nature of mankind, to penetrate the source of all knowledge and, above all, to experience genuine intimacy.

My nagging feeling was reinforced when she began to attend more of Dr. Farsante's seminars. She urged me to go as well. When I refused, she carefully elaborated a number of Dr. Farsante's more positive characteristics, many of which I did not possess. Gradually, comparisons between my psychic abilities and those of Dr. Farsante became the overriding theme of our relationship. Slowly I came to realize that there is no short cut, no switch to turn love on or off. Rather, it moves through stages. Much as flour does on its way to becoming fresh-baked bread, love must be massaged and kept at the right temperature lest it become a cold grey lump of dough.

Consequently I again visited Professor Aguilar. "Your strategy has worked," I told her. "I have found a companion who fulfills my desires, but I have the troublesome notion that she is not attracted to me for my best qualities, and that may be the crack in the foundation that will cause the whole edifice of our relationship to crumble, similar to the way the carefully constructed face of a lady disintegrates in the rain."

The professor smiled. "Of course she isn't attracted to you for your best qualities," she said. "Your best qualities are as well hidden as flaws in a starlet's complexion. What she sees in you is a reflection of herself."

"But will that not keep us from equally enjoying our relationship, and will not the one who enjoys it least cause tiny seeds of discontent to germinate?"

"Let me explain something," Professor Aguilar said. "Two cars travelling side by side will register the same velocity. But if one is in high gear and the other in low the motors will be racing at different rates. You and Prana may be like those cars. You both could be moving at the same speed in your relationship, but perhaps your motor is a bit sluggish compared to hers."

"I don't think my motor is sluggish," I said. "I understand what you're saying, yet I still have a concern. Prana spends every waking moment and all of her energy searching for something else in life. She looks for answers to great problems in an irrational manner. My concern is not that our motors run at different speeds but that we are driving in the same direction. I say this because I believe she has a secret and unhealthy fixation on Dr. Farsante."

"Why do you think that?" Professor Aguilar asked.

"Her quest is to find true intimacy and she thinks it resides in Dr. Farsante's teaching. She knows that she can transform her life by altering her attitude and behaviour, yet it is my attitude and behaviour she endeavours to change. I find this difficult as the part of me she wishes to modify varies from moment to moment. Ironically, her search for intimacy is preventing us from finding it."

"But it takes two," Professor Aguilar said. "Do you think Dr. Farsante is also interested in Prana?"

"Yes I do. She is to attend a private workshop with him where he will probe her capacity for a close relationship. The workshop, for which she will pay a large fee, is to be conducted at his seaside villa. I am not invited. She is to bring only herself, an open attitude, and exotic lingerie."

My tale was stopped by a burst of mirth from Adriana. "It sounds like Dr. Farsante was not the naïve side of the triangle. Did it happen? Did Prana accompany him to his home at the beach?"

"Yes she did, and she never returned. She stayed with him until he spied the next set of curves on his personal highway. Later she started a Utopian community somewhere in the mountains. I did not see her for years . . . but recently I was able to locate her as part of my research into my own life."

"Tell me about her," Adriana demanded. "Was she still interested in quick and simple fixes to age-old problems?"

"She is like most who look for easy answers," I said. "They search until they die or alternatively, they grow cynical because of the lack of meaning in what they find. Prana has not escaped that fate."

❧

She swept into Don Emilio's restaurant accompanied by a man who looked familiar. At first glance it seemed she had not aged but as she came closer I realized that she had travelled a number of routes on her journey to her current appearance. An attempt had been made to remove facial wrinkles and it had left her skin stretched so that blood vessels made blue, spider-like patterns, which she had attempted to hide by liberally applying makeup. Unfortunately the motion required by speech had caused the makeup to crack so that it resembled pavement after an earthquake. Below the boundary of her latest alteration, the folds on her neck resembled pleats on a Scottish kilt and bore the same mixture of colours. Her breasts had been adjusted so that they acted as signposts to two ancient realms — the right pointed toward heaven and the left waved at the underworld. Her lips had been expanded to the extent that they had lost symmetry and now served the same function as a billboard by drawing attention away from the surrounding landscape. Each of her fingers was weighted by rings, and her earrings — which were the colour, shape, and size of a large pizza — pulled her earlobes below her shoulders. Her purple dress was clearly designed to repel wild animals.

Her companion was greying and prematurely bald with skin the colour of stale bread. I stood as they approached and this diverted his attention from the task of reining in his abdomen. He exhaled and an apron of flab unrolled over his belt, much the way a tarpaulin is set free to keep a baseball diamond dry. His jowls jiggled and his breath came in loud rasps as if he had just run a five kilometre race.

They sat and he began tossing taco chips and salsa into his mouth faster than he could swallow. The excess soon dribbled from his chin to be absorbed by the table cloth. I recognized Raoul.

"The last time I saw you was during an emergency in Professor Aguilar's office," I said.

"Yes," he answered, wiping his chin with the back of his hand. "I was employed by Professor Aguilar to be on standby in case of emergencies. I earned my salary. Coping with as many as four emergencies a day was strenuous."

I found it difficult to reminisce with Prana while Raoul held her hand and grinned at me with salsa running over his chin. So I enquired about people we both knew. "Whatever became of the professor?" I asked. "Her office has been closed for years. Did she move from the city?"

"Yes, she did," Prana replied. "You are out of touch. Do you not know that she and Dr. Farsante were married? Both left their respective professions to become born again radio evangelists. Every Sunday they heal sick and maimed people who call in to their radio show and describe various afflictions. Such is their skill, that from hundreds of kilometres away, they have been known to make a crippled man walk or hemorrhoids disappear. They are so popular that their phone lines are frequently jammed. Occasionally the telephone operator becomes confused and they heal the wrong affliction. Once I heard them help a baby girl who was suffering from an enlarged prostate . . . and just last week they mistakenly treated a blind man for impotence. The poor man was gracious, though. He said that although he remained unable to see, he no longer needed a white cane to poke in front of him as he walked."

"Interesting," I said. "Tell me, have you managed to find the true intimacy you were seeking?"

"Intimacy is just another word for honesty," she said. "It must come from both parties. That's why I left, although it wasn't your fault. It was me who wasn't honest. I wanted you to be my conduit to a metaphysical understanding of the universe, which I thought I needed in order to experience love. When I discovered that the metaphysics of a doughnut was beyond your capability, I had to leave."

"I don't understand . . . the metaphysics of a doughnut?"

"Exactly! I will give you credit, however. All of my previous lovers treated intimacy like a contagious disease, but you weren't afraid. You were just driving in a different direction."

"What do you mean, a different direction?"

"Don't get me wrong. You were visibly normal, you were clean, you wore good, though outdated clothes, and you had a few social skills. It was simply a case of too much and too little. I had too much hope and you had too little promise. You didn't recognize my need . . . and not recognizing it meant that you could not fill it."

"You didn't answer my question," I said. "Did you ever find the intimacy you sought?"

"In a way," she said. "Sexuality is an exalted place where intimacy sometimes hides. Raoul helps me look for it." She patted his hand. "Don't you, snuggle cheeks?"

Raoul chuckled, prompting more food to seek safety on the table cloth. Prana leaned over, kissed him and began licking the salsa from his chin. Both became so engrossed in this activity that they didn't notice when I called for the bill.

At the door I glanced back. She was feeding him the taco chips, one-by-one, carefully inserting them so that the salsa stayed on the chip and his chin remained dry.

❧

Adriana snorted. "You're slower than a slumbering sloth," she said. "You lost before the game started, my dried-up doughnut friend. When Prana said that you didn't recognize her need, she meant that you didn't listen. Listening isn't just for ears. There must be action. A need exists only if it's not met, just as I feel the need to sleep only when I'm not sleeping . . . or when I listen to you."

I poured another drink and dialed my listening down to monitor.

"Intimacy is never repellent like warm is never cold," she continued. "A couple not only must trust each other enough to tell everything, each must trust enough to listen. Effort is required. That's why intimate relationships are fragile and that's why most marital alliances are not filled with ecstasy and happiness. They take too much work."

She leaned back, held up her glass and gazed through it. "Quite apart from all that," she said, "you might have found everlasting love if only you had learned to talk with your mouth full. Nevertheless, my crumbling taco chip, I think you were lucky that Prana left you. You could have spent the rest of your life having your chin licked."

I took a sip of brandy and changed the subject. "It's amazing how Professor Aguilar and Dr. Farsante ended up together when they started so far apart."

Adriana sniffed. "They didn't go half a block. The overlap between what a professional counsellor doesn't know and what a phoney healer doesn't know is quite large. So is the intersection of what they both will refuse to admit they don't know. They have more in common than they are generally given credit for."

"You must explain yourself," I said.

She sniffed again. "Think of it this way. If love, happiness, or prosperity can be gained by anyone who believes in the ability of a therapist, isn't lack of any of those things the fault of the sufferer for not having a strong enough belief? This is the fallacy perpetrated by all charlatans."

Later, I made my way home to bed. Adriana is right about one thing. I had been lucky. If she is also right about another then I am destined to end my days outside of an intimate relationship. Work of any kind has never been my strong suit.

Adriana's Story

I BELIEVE PERSONAL STORIES ARE LIKE LEVERS. We use them to pry our lives into alignment with the world's expectations. We all need stories. Can you feature a person without one? She would have no identity — no face to show the world.

Adriana's story reveals many faces. In the time that we have been neighbours she has confided numerous details of her life although she wishes them kept private. I will now pass them to you exactly as she told them to me.

Although she is not as old as I, Adriana too would face severe drought if the only water left was that yet to flow under her bridge. She began life in an itinerant fashion, born into a carnival family where her father was a trick rider and her mother a tamer of big cats. She has carried the characteristics of these parental occupations into later life. Much of her time is spent trying to either trick or tame me.

Her childhood and youth were spent performing for audiences in every part of the country. While her parents were fine citizens they had little time for her as she was growing up. Sideshow performers became her family and her teachers. She has fond memories of Esmeralda, the two-headed lady who kept her extra head and the mirrors that went with it stored in a box under her trailer. "Each of her heads had different personalities," Adriana recalls. "When I was small I marvelled at how unalike they were. The head in the box was pale with yellow teeth and mousy grey hair. It wore no makeup and never spoke. When performing it sipped water from a glass while Esmeralda's other head, covered in rouge and bright lipstick, smoked cigarettes and talked to the audience. That head was loud, swore a lot, and frequently drank whiskey."

Esmeralda taught Adriana that life is illusion. "We damn well don't know anything for sure," she said. "Maybe it's all a dream and we don't really exist. *I think, therefore I am*, is meaningless. It depends on which head I am using. Many of my best ideas originate in the box under my trailer."

A recent disagreement illustrates a further aspect of Adriana's early education. I am not a good looking man and the Lord has not blessed me with a pleasing personality. Adriana says I am difficult and bad tempered and she frequently comments on my appearance. "If handsome is as handsome does then you should be an inert object," she crows. Once she told me that if good looks came in limousines then I would have arrived on a burro.

"Life is compensation," I told her. "I have been able to offset my lack of looks and personality by developing an impeccable moral nature and a set of ethical principles which are pure and which remain as fresh and uncontaminated as if they had been purchased yesterday. It's a credit to my upright temperament that I have lived by these principles for most of my adult life with only occasional slippage."

"You must be thinking with Esmeralda's second head," she replied. "Morality and principles should be like a pair of shoes . . . they should fit the same way every day."

"Not so," I said. "I have observed that principles and morality are primarily products of circumstance and that circumstance is generally within our control although, occasionally, fate or the Lord may prescribe some condition that necessitates bending our actions in unanticipated directions, causing compensating twists to both principles and morality. It is precisely this moral flexibility that has made me a superior lover, allowed me the latitude I needed to perfect the romantic art, and given me the ability to adapt to my partner's expectations in much the same manner that a chameleon changes colour. It has always set me apart."

"Nonsense!" she said. "Morals and principles should be rigid and unbending as if written in stone. If the Lord meant principles to be pliable he would have given Moses ten suggestions, and He would have written them in chalk . . . on a slate."

It should come as no surprise to learn that Adriana received many of her early lessons from an old carnival performer named Brittle Man who used to stiffen his body between two chairs while weights were placed on his stomach. "He never even bent," she said.

"That's because too little weight was applied, my decorous dumbbell. More pounds and he would have been called Elastic Man.

Travelling did not allow for formal education and Adriana has never attended school. All of her knowledge is the result of hearsay and therefore inadmissible when we argue, although she says that by the time of her middle teens she had completed degrees in fire-eating, juggling, clowning, and trapeze artisting.

These first steps toward an independent nature were already complete when she fell into a severe emotional crisis. An adolescent crush proved tragic. She had been learning the intricacies of sword swallowing from a veteran performer when, quite by accident, she found herself in love with her teacher. More often than not an infatuation at her age would have passed in the normal fashion but the situation was complicated. The sword swallower's name was Alana and, when not swallowing swords, she doubled as the carnival's bearded lady.

Unsure of what an estrogen-based relationship might mean in terms of her gender role, Adriana became host to a giant identity battle. Alana was tall, full figured, and had a luxuriant growth of red facial hair. Her image dominated Adriana's thoughts, causing an internal storm of such intensity that it came near to capsizing her mental stability. Fortunately, the situation resolved itself when the carnival was raided by the police. Many of the midway performers were charged with fraud and it was revealed that Alana, the bearded lady, was actually Alan, the bearded man. At first Adriana felt only relief. The issue of her sexual preference was resolved. However, Alan was forced to flee to avoid incarceration. She never saw him again, but to this day she has a soft spot for individuals of either sex who contend with the world from the backside of a bewhiskered countenance.

Following closely on the heels of relief, Adriana fell into a pit of despair. How could she ever love again? "In my head I had committed my entire being to Alan," she said. "I could not forsake his memory. My love wasn't like an old man's erection — it didn't go away."

"You mistook a mouse for an elephant," I said. "Because love is too complex for a neophyte it was easy for you to misconstrue your infatuation. You cannot know a fine vintage if you've never tasted wine. Even I, a seasoned veteran, occasionally find love perplexing."

"I understand exactly," she said. "When you speak, I sometimes mistake excrement for fertilizer."

I ignored her remark and stroked the stubble on my chin. "So what happened, my whisker-loving wench? How long did you pine for lost love?"

"Actually, it was amazing how quickly my love boat overcame its momentum and changed course. I rebounded but I jumped too far. Perhaps as a result of emotional trauma, I leapt into my first marriage. I began a pursuit of the carnival's strong man, Antonio Baricco. He was a tanned giant with rippling muscles and a black handlebar moustache sprouting from a rugged face. I particularly liked the way he looked in his leopard skin tights."

The pursuit of Antonio was difficult. Dressed in his tights, he spent all of his off-stage hours in front of a large mirror that he had mounted on the side of his trailer. He always began by smiling at the mirror. The smile gradually faded as his eyes took on the intensity of a goaltender poised for a soccer ball. Staring into the mirror, he flexed and posed. Then he posed and flexed, and whispered to his image, gradually increasing the volume until he was shouting epithets, daring the mirror to throw back a less than perfect reflection. Daily, Adriana paraded by dressed in provocative attire, but he had eyes only for the facsimile that watched from the mirror.

Adriana has never been known for reticence when it comes to achieving a goal. She studied Antonio's schedule. He broke away from his narcissistic exercise for only two reasons: to put on his regular act during which he performed feats of incredible strength for admiring audiences, and to chew handfuls of vitamins, pep pills and minerals which he washed down with litres of health tonics.

"I remember the day well," she explained. "While he was performing, I substituted pure alcohol for one of his tonics. Then I hid behind a tree near his trailer and waited while guilt nibbled at my conscience. Above me, leafy branches framed patches of sky — blue paintings that hosted soaring white seagulls. Other birds flew in and out of the paintings. One swooped low and sat on a branch, a black crow that cocked his head and accused me with beady eyes.

"Antonio was already in a rubbery state when he arrived to begin preening. When he staggered and almost collapsed, I rushed to help put him to bed in his trailer. He weighed over 200 pounds and it was difficult to remove the tights. What followed was not what I expected. He seemed to have the right idea but every time we came close to achieving what I had envisioned he began talking to himself — at least to parts of himself. Not the parts you would imagine, but to his biceps, which he had named as if they were children. He called the right Romeo and the left Juliet. 'Romeo,' he muttered, 'What for are thou? Juliet, you are neither hand nor foot . . . and I'm weak and loose in the head.'"

"How long did he keep up that nonsense?" I asked.

"Until he fell asleep, right after he sang a lullaby to each of his muscles. He was snoring when I left. However, I accomplished my purpose. Someone told him that it was me who put him to bed and he came to say thanks. We went out and two weeks later we were married. I was his first date, his first girlfriend, and his first wife.

"But problems surfaced as soon as he realized that I intended to share star billing with his pectorals. It turned out that he loved only those parts of his body that drew ooh's and aah's from the crowd. The part that was crucial for our wedding night he considered as useless as ears on a deaf man — it had never brought him accolades. There was not a musician alive who could have made that organ play.

"It took weeks to consummate the marriage and that only after I stole his leopard skin tights, recited poetry to Romeo, and told bedtime stories to Juliet. I also spent hours telling the apparatus he considered useless that it was a muscle-bound god. However, it was only after I set up an exercise schedule for it that I got any reaction."

"So what caused the break-up?"

"I realized that I would never play first fiddle in his orchestra — a marriage certificate is not a deed of sexual ownership. We divorced. In spite of my planning, I was left with only a small dent in my virginity but with a firm resolve to have a major fender-bender as soon as possible. The good news is that I avoided being stuck with support payments for Romeo and Juliet."

"You do make mistakes," I said. "First a mouse for an elephant and then you confused a burro for a horse. Infatuation is not love and neither is lust, although it is closer to it in an evolutionary sense. Lust is merely static that makes it difficult for one's sexual antenna to bring in a clear broadcast."

"You illustrate your own point," she said. "It's like trying to comprehend gibberish. However, you have reminded me of something. One of the workers who set up and dismantled the attractions was an indigenous man. He was ancient and had travelled with the carnival for so long that no one remembered where he came from. He told me he had been a revered storyteller in his tribe. As you know, it is the storytellers in a society who portray and make sense of the world. His name was Torquetri and I remember him talking about love and lust. He told me this story:

In the beginning there was confusion with bits and pieces of things everywhere, floating around and bumping into other bits and pieces. There were two deities, He-God and She-God, but they were inexperienced and didn't know what to do. So chaos reigned and it was only after many eternities that things began to sort themselves out. Eventually the right pieces stuck together and the first women appeared. Then it started to rain. Some of the women became unglued and fell apart. Concerned, the gods put them back together but they were in a hurry, had no blueprint, and so made mistakes. These mistakes they called men. That is why today some parts of men fit together with parts of women.

Occasionally, She-God became bored. For Her own amusement, She removed pieces from what had already been created. Her favourite pastime was to steal the appendage from a man and then laugh while the man searched frantically for his missing part. However, some men were no fun — they didn't search. These men reconciled themselves to their loss by moving into the biggest cave, carrying the heaviest club or brandishing the longest spear. Whenever that happened, She-God, in a fit of pique, would give life to the stolen item. That is why two types of males walk the earth — those with no penis but intellect intact, and penises that stand upright with no brain attached. The latter tend to frequent bars and sporting events. For ease of description I refer to these two men as Tiny Tim and Willie. Thus, She-God set into motion that which frustrates women to this day — the fruitless search for something that doesn't exist, and the slow realization of why — that a whole man is simply the simultaneous embodiment of flesh and lust.

He-God was envious that She-God was having all the fun. In a fanciful attempt to imitate Her pleasure, He selected a woman, removed the part called reason and breathed life into it. Thus, there began to be seen on earth, two kinds of females — those with reason alone and those who represent unscathed desire but lack the sense to mitigate it. To keep the latter amused, He-God invented diets and make-up. For ease of description I call these two women Chastity and Muffy. He-God looked at what He had wrought, saw that it was good and then, utilizing His recent experience, He moved on to create pre-nuptial agreements. Thus, He-God set into motion that which frustrates men to this day — the pointless search for something that doesn't exist — a woman who is restrained on the street but wanton in the bedroom.

After six days, the gods tired of their play. They moved to Saskatchewan to be with their own kind, and abandoned humans to their own devices forever. From that day, four types of people have roamed the world meeting, mating, and marrying.

The results of these liaisons are predictable: when Chastity meets Tiny Tim the only possible result is platonic romance with each secretly wondering why others have more fun, while the outcome of Tim encountering Muffy is a short frustrating affair. When Wandering Willie finds Chastity, the consequence is an unstable marriage, but the upshot when he stumbles over Muffy is always fun — fun that lasts right up until the advent of morning sickness."

"An interesting story," I said. "But what is the point?"

"The point," she retorted, "is that I now know why you live alone in such a big house."

Adriana has spent an inordinate amount of time dancing the bridal waltz but I won't bore you with the details of her ensuing two marriages, both of which occurred when she was still young. Neither lasted long. She says they were as memorable as tepid weather. Her next nuptial deserves mention, however, as it caused her to leave the midway and resulted in her eventually becoming my next door neighbour.

"By the time I acquired my fourth husband the conjugal bed no longer held mystery," she said. "I had misplaced my virginity so many times that Marco Polo couldn't have found it.

"The marriage was a terrible mistake. His name was El Cuchillo and he had a knife-throwing act. As well as knives, he liked to throw his weight around. I'm no cowering cutie but he was a big man and I did not fare well. However, he did teach me his art. I proved adept and soon the pupil's skill surpassed that of her teacher. I became the star of the show and my bully-boy husband moved into the background as my assistant.

That's when the accident happened. The act always resulted in calls for an encore. To fill this demand I strapped him to a large wooden wheel and set it rotating. I then stepped back and threw sharp knives into the wheel until they completely outlined the perimeter of his body. The climax occurred when I threw the final knife high up between his legs. Unfortunately I missed and El Cuchillo suddenly became eligible for service as a soprano in a ladies' choir. Rather than sing, we divorced and he quietly slipped away to live in a facility that housed infirm and elderly performers, becoming one of the few people ever to run away from the circus to join a home."

"It sounds like he deserved his fate, my neutering Nellie. I like to dine in fine restaurants but I don't choose items from the menu that I find distasteful. Why is it that you persisted in jumping into less-than-satisfactory marital situations?"

Adriana grimaced. "Like many women, I was raised to believe that happiness can only occur if you stare over the cereal box at the same person for all of eternity and that this state of conformity is the only heaven available here on earth. What I didn't know was that a man is most happy when he experiences only selected fragments of a marriage. He wants someone to prepare meals but not to prepare a schedule for his day off; he desires to share his bed but not his secrets or his closet; he wishes for an admirer to gaze up at him but doesn't want anyone peering into his bank book; he wants a hostess to entertain his friends but not a new companion on the golf course. Learning this took a great deal of trial and a lot of error."

I have already told you the story of Adriana's final marriage and how she came to acquire the house next door. I have also revealed our brief visit to Passion Mountain and why it is that we no longer make that trek. What I have not explained is how Adriana fits into my life and why it is that I would become a sorry soul were she to leave.

Adriana is one of the few women to whom I can actually talk.

Praying for a Relationship

ADRIANA COMPLETED HER STORY AND CARRIED her glass to the kitchen, a signal that I should go home. But I was not about to leave. She waited for a moment and then poured us each another brandy. "What is it, my cute cadaver? Has *rigor mortis* set in?"

"No it hasn't. Your story has triggered a memory, an event that happened long before I learned that a mature person prays for a relationship rather than an orgasm."

She handed me my drink. "Let's hear it. I might as well be entertained while I chaperone."

❧

In those days, I frequently found strong drink a pleasant alternative when God ignored my prayers. One particular evening, while riding my favourite bar stool, I ruminated on the distance that my life had traversed since I had last enjoyed the sheer anticipatory pleasure of even the possibility of an erotic encounter. Wallowing in self-pity, I decided that even a quick glimpse of a naked woman would be infinitely more gratifying than the full frontal nudity displayed by the ice-cubes in my glass. Consequently, I proceeded to Bronco Bananas, a nearby nightclub that advertised itself by displaying large posters of exotic women in various stages of undress.

I entered, acquired a table near the stage, and ordered a drink without ice. Soon after I sat down, a lady, dressed in a fashion that told me she was one of the performers, sashayed across the room. She was tall, full bodied and had long red hair. As she passed, my mouth acted on its own. 'Hello beautiful,' it said.

"Hi yourself, gorgeous," she replied. "Mind if I sit down?"

"Please do. You're as welcome as a cloud burst in a drought. Can I buy you a drink?"

"I don't drink before a show, but thank you anyway. Please go ahead."

I ordered another. Soon our words flowed at a brisk pace and we began enjoying ourselves.

"My name's Barbie," she said. "Have you seen my act?"

"No, I haven't. My name's Alberto and I can't wait."

"Do you have a wife or a girlfriend?"

I'm afraid that I have been blessed with neither for a very long time."

"Then what do you do for pleasure, Alberto? Surely a dashing individual such as yourself has little need to sit alone in an establishment where the only audience participation is wishful thinking."

I felt my chest swell. Clearly, Barbie was someone who recognized talent. Our conversation became intimate and she suggested we move to a booth for privacy. I ordered another drink for myself and a tonic water for her.

As soon as we were in the booth, she leaned over and fastened her lips on mine. Her eyes shone through her eyelashes and I felt her hand pass across my lap. It did this a few times and then rested there rhythmically squeezing the front of my trousers.

She broke the kiss. "Who is this gentleman that stands in the presence of a lady? Does he have a name?"

"I like to call him, Old Faithful," I said. "Although he doesn't erupt on a regular basis."

✄

Adriana had been trying to erupt on a regular basis since I started my story. She found her opening. "Old Faithful, my backside! He should be called, Sense of Humour because his main role in life is to amuse." She punctuated her statement with a loud bray and a spray. I ignored the former and wiped away the latter before I continued.

✄

Barbie smiled, displaying even white teeth. I felt the unzip before she disappeared, out of sight below the table. I kept drinking and tried to look nonchalant, hoping other patrons would think that she had gone to the bathroom. Because of my advanced state of imaginary anticipation she did not have to stay out of sight for very long.

I ordered another drink to recover. "I feel that I should reciprocate," I said.

She raised her eyes as she applied fresh lipstick. "I'd love that but my show is about to begin. I'll take a raincheck." She gave me a kiss, stuck her tongue in my ear and said, "let me know what you think of my performance."

Her dance was elegant and daring at the same time. She owned the stage, cavorting, teasing, exotic, erotic — every man in the place lusted. She disrobed while using a large fan and her long red hair to conceal her exposure, offering the audience only brief glimpses of an exquisite body. I felt myself falling in love.

At the finale she came to centre stage, and removed the fan, the red hair . . . and her breasts! Barbie was a man!

I was stunned. How could this be? I had no advance warning that I was a homosexual.

He exited the stage and the next act, a comedian with a trained monkey, started his routine. I was curious. What was there about myself, an individual whose gender bucket was overflowing with heterosexuality, that would cause Barbie to think that I drove on both sides of the street. I waited but he didn't return. When I enquired, I was told that it had been his last show and that he had gone home.

I, too, went home but I was unable to sleep. The experience had not been unpleasant. An old refrain of my father's replayed itself in my memory: *You can be anything that you aspire to.* I had always aspired to be heterosexual but it wasn't working for me. I thought, *why not aspire to something else?*

The following evening I bypassed my usual watering hole and returned to Bronco Bananas to see Barbie. We sat in the same booth. "Barbie is my stage name. My real name is Benito. How did you like my act?" he asked.

"You have influenced me and now I want you to teach me. I have decided to become a homosexual."

He laughed. "I'd love to but I'm afraid it may be impossible. You either are or you aren't. It's like becoming an Irishman. You can't just decide to be one. You must start out that way."

"I disagree. Anyone can become Irish. All you have to do is drink more. I think it's like religion. I know Catholics who have become Protestants and I've even met a former Anglican who became a Buddhist."

"That's not the same thing at all. You're mixing grapefruit and mangos. Think about it. A Japanese can't become a Yugoslav."

"Okay, I'll give you that."

"But what if one of your parents is Irish and one is Japanese. Then you could be Buddhist or Catholic as the spirit moves you. Isn't that the same?"

Benito shrugged his shoulders, signalling boredom with the direction of our conversation.

We agreed to disagree. I stayed to see his show again and he reluctantly began my lesson. Afterwards, I went home to bed where I dreamed that I was a Yugoslavian Buddhist.

Adriana stopped me. "I didn't know that you had grazed in that pasture."

"You may not believe this from someone whose cargo of virility threatens to spring its lid, but I can kick a soccer ball with either foot, my personal ship has listed to both starboard and port, and I can sit anywhere on the bus — the destination doesn't change."

"But I see no evidence that you adopted that lifestyle. I've never seen you in a cardigan, your shirts aren't pink and you hardly ever wear tight pants."

"That's a stereotype I never adopted. However, I did apprentice for a while."

"Did you tire of Benito?"

"No, it was he who tired of me. He met a policeman from Texas and moved away. I didn't know how to find another playmate so I abandoned the effort. Besides, I had been much more attracted to Barbie than I was to Benito. I guess I just wasn't a good student, the experiment didn't work. I figured out that I belong on the traditional side of the divide."

Adriana pursed her lips. "What do you mean? There is no divide. You sound like one of those idiots who spouts invective from the safety of a pulpit. You have learned little about human sexuality."

"No divide? Even Benito said you are or you aren't. You must explain yourself, my preachy pontificator."

"It's impossible to categorize. Human sexuality is on a continuum from absolute heterosexual to absolute homosexual. Everyone fits somewhere on that continuum and every space is filled. The only way to make a category is to create a stereotype and once you accept a stereotype, then you are less than a millimetre away from being a bigot."

"Are you saying that categories are useless?"

"Not at all. I'm saying that there is nothing traditional about any sexual role."

She yawned, again signalling that it was time for me to leave. The path home was lit by a pale moon. Adriana had a point. What we call tradition is simply a way to classify past behaviour, in many cases condemning us to repeat the intolerance, prejudice, and bigotry that, long ago, should have been consigned to a historical incinerator.

Words Can Make You Happy

THE TILES ON ADRIANA'S PATIO WERE still warm from the afternoon sun and a rising moon had given them a rose glaze. I had exhausted her tolerance for my story and my own tolerance for hers. We sipped expensive brandy and settled into a comfortable silence, listening to the night birds and the raucous music of summer cicadas. Adriana closed one eye and squinted at me through her glass. "Are you happy, old man?" she asked.

A personal query that isn't followed by an insult is unlike her and for a few minutes I was unable to reply. A small fruit bat, more shadow than substance, fluttered by barely visible against the black bramble hill that rose behind Adriana's house. I hesitated because the question was not flippant and deserved a serious answer.

"Well, are you?" she repeated.

"I'm considering my reply. I haven't thought of happiness in a long time. Let me tip the hammock and ask you. Is your existence satisfactory? Do you ache for that which never happened?"

I removed my sandals to feel the warm tiles and leaned back. She had started us on a new path and I intended to enjoy the outing.

"I asked you first," she said.

"I'm thinking, my demanding diva. I'm thinking that you must first tell me what you mean by happy. It could be anything. Do I have enough to eat? An adequate dwelling? Enough money? Am I free from sickness? Am I pleased with my role in life? Do I have friends? Have all my love wounds healed? Your question begs for definition."

I took a satisfied breath. I might not be able to stop Adriana's mental horses but often I can slow them down.

"I agree that happiness is a less than rigorous term," she said. "How would you define it?"

"Perhaps it's found in leading an easy life — one with no difficulties."

"Not so," she answered. "I once thought I'd be happy if I had no problems."

"And?" I asked.

"When the lucky day arrived, I was bored to silliness. To put flavour into my life I began to create predicaments."

"Such as?"

"It started when I introduced a gentleman of my acquaintance to the young lady who was my hairdresser. They fell in love, married and began raising a family. He was a barber and together they opened a salon which did very well."

"It sounds idyllic. What caused your predicament?"

"I took pleasure in the fact that I had introduced them and considered what it was that made them happy. I determined that it was their common interest in hair."

"Go on," I said.

"I believed that I had solved the riddle of attraction and love. The key was to have something tangible in common. To relieve my boredom I started a match-making service. My approach was very scientific."

I refilled my glass and settled in for the duration. She had flown to another story and I had soared after her like an airplane chases its propeller. "Tell me," I said.

"It wasn't complicated. I created random lists of words and then asked each client to select the ones that had meaning or held interest for him or her. Then I matched individuals on the basis of the common or related words they chose. For example, I introduced people who had picked words like style, gown, soiree, tuxedo, fashion, chic, elegant, flair, and so on — you get the idea?"

"Yes I do. Did it work?"

"At first all went well. Then I began to encounter problems."

"What kind of problems?"

"It began simply enough. My first complaint was from a female athlete, a long distance runner."

"Yes?"

"She had chosen from a list that contained words like foot, socks, running shoe, insole, sneaker, high heels and hosiery. I introduced her to someone who had selected similar words. It worked perfectly. They hit it off and, for awhile, they were inseparable."

"What went wrong?"

"Unfortunately, he turned out to be a foot fetishist."

"I see. Did he spend all his time caressing her feet and getting her to model for him in high heels or white rubber boots?"

"No, that wasn't it. She could have lived with that. It wasn't *her* feet that sparked his interest."

"You mean she had a rival?"

"Yes, she did. His obsession lay elsewhere."

"I don't understand."

"It's simple. Of the billions of people in the world, he was fascinated with only one."

"No wonder your match didn't work. He was already in a relationship."

"Yes, he was . . . and a very peculiar one, too."

"What do you mean, peculiar?"

"Of all the feet he could have chosen, he was attracted to only one."

"One person and one foot. Different . . . but it doesn't sound that peculiar."

"You don't understand. The relationship was with his own foot . . . the left one. He worshipped it and wrote poems to it. He often left home wearing only one shoe."

"Why only one shoe?"

"He felt secure when he could glance down and see his beloved at the end of his left leg."

"No wonder they broke up."

"It wasn't that. She said she could have borne the embarrassment of going dancing with someone wearing one shoe."

"What then? What caused their break up?"

"Her athletic training began to suffer and she started to lose races."

"Aha . . . I understand. It must have been psychologically damaging to play second fiddle to a left foot. She would be unable to concentrate on her training."

"Wrong again. The reason she lost races was because of pulled muscles."

"Pulled muscles?"

"Yes, pulled because of the position she assumed so he could caress his foot as they made love."

"I see."

"They split up and I was forced to give their money back."

"Your idea seems good. Did you encounter other setbacks?"

"Many of them."

"What happened?"

"I analysed the situation to find out. I determined that it was because I was using only nouns on my lists, words that didn't necessarily have much to do with human affairs. So I created other lists — lists that used more appropriate words — words that had to do with relationships and emotions. I reasoned that a common interest in these types of words would bring together people who were compatible."

"Your approach sounds reasonable."

"I ran into trouble when I introduced Felix and Katrina, based on that approach. They started well but they grew to disagree on almost everything."

"I don't understand."

"Neither did I. So I questioned them. I discovered that not everyone interprets words the same way."

"For example?"

"One of the words was *vulnerable*. When I asked what the word meant to her, Katrina said that she felt vulnerable when she opened herself completely to another person, as she had done with Felix by disclosing the inner recesses of her heart."

"I see nothing wrong so far."

"Hold on, my impatient imbecile. I questioned Felix separately. He said he felt vulnerable whenever he bet on a strange horse."

"So they didn't see eye to eye on one word. Surely they agreed on others."

"Not many. They both chose the word *pleasure*. Katrina felt pleasure when she had the opportunity to luxuriate in sensuous surroundings. To Felix, pleasure was pizza and a cold beer."

"Are there others?"

"Many! Take *communication* . . . to Katrina it meant sharing her most profound feelings and emotions. Felix had difficulty with this one until I reminded him that intimacy is impossible without communication."

"Everyone communicates. Did he give an example?"

'Yes, he did. He said that he had once complimented Katrina on a personal level, and though her response had been intimate, it had also been unorthodox."

"What was the nature of his compliment?"

"He told Katrina that, viewed from the rear, she wasn't all that much larger than his last girlfriend."

"You say her response was intimate?"

"Yes it was. She kicked him in the testicles."

"I understand the problem that might cause."

"You haven't heard half of it. Another word was *entertainment*. Katrina considered herself entertained if she attended a good play or movie, or if she heard a great tenor."

"Surely Felix didn't disagree with that."

"No, he didn't disagree. He said that was fine, but to him entertainment was having a front row seat at a strip club."

"Interesting. Tell me more, my miscast matchmaker."

"*Feelings*. How could they not agree on *feelings*? But they did. Katrina said her feelings were an expression of her innermost state. Felix said his feelings were what got hurt when his friend didn't buy the next round."

"Surely that's all."

"No, I'll give you one more. *Fear* was a word on my list. Katrina said that her biggest fear was that Felix would leave her for someone else. When I asked Felix what his greatest fear was, he said, 'Spiders'."

"Enough! I see your problem. Did you quit the business? Did you learn anything about happiness?"

"Yes to both. I learned that the absence of difficulty in life can cause us to create predicaments, and that perhaps the key to happiness is not a problem-free existence but how we respond to problems when they arise."

"How we respond doesn't matter if there is no positive effect."

"Maybe and maybe not. Suppose the response to a problem is to live in denial. That could have a positive or negative effect depending on circumstances. Maybe there could be short term denial for long term gain."

Here we go again, I thought. Out loud I said, "Give me an example, my dim darling of definitions."

"You'll identify with this one, oh limp lever of love," she said

I refilled my glass. From the corner of my eye I saw the fruit bat making its return trip.

"One of my husbands was well under-endowed. Living with him was like having an extra little finger with no sense of direction and the consistency of spaghetti, if you know what I mean. However, he had other qualities, not the least of which was that what he lacked in certain departments was more than compensated for by the size of his bank account. Besides, I cared for him and he for me, a situation so rare that I determined to do everything I could to make our marriage work."

"What did you do?"

"I lived in denial. I pretended and then eventually convinced myself that he was the best lover on the face of the earth. It was a form of self-hypnosis. Of course reality hibernated under the bed and I was frequently frustrated."

"That doesn't sound good. Where's the long term gain in that?"

"He was a sensitive, intelligent man and he determined to do something about his problem. He embarked on a rigorous learning program. His ultimate goal was to acquire a degree in love with a major in Adriana. He proved a magnificent student and graduated *magna cum laude*. I won't elaborate except to say that he would have made a wonderful doctor — he knew enough to treat the whole patient."

"What is your point, my little pleasure pot?" I asked.

"The point, my inept idiot, is that denial paid off and I ended up with a great lover."

Great, but not the greatest, I thought. "Where is he? Surely you didn't leave him."

"No, I didn't, but I made a grievous error. I told my best friend and she told her friends. The next thing I know, I'm engaged in a frantic competition, the intensity of which has never been equalled at an Olympiad. My best friend won and she ran away with my husband."

"Okay, you've convinced me. We can set up defences to preserve our well-being but they're no good if they spell ruin rather than redemption."

"Exactly," she said. "I think our lives exist on a spectrum that runs from miserable to elated and there is a happy point on that spectrum where each of us is most contented. When we are pushed away from that point in either direction, we take the action necessary to return. Sometimes we overshoot. Moving back and forth helps clarify our self-image, much like adjusting binoculars clarifies the image we see through the lens . . . and remember, our adjustments also range from bad to good."

Now we're adjusting binoculars, I thought. *The way Adriana's mental kite spins in the wind, we could end up flying a jet aircraft.* Aloud I said, "Explain yourself, my ill-focused fiddlehead."

"It's like piloting a fast plane," she said. "Everything must be kept in equilibrium. Any adjustment we make could be balanced and mature, but it could also be psychotic. In between those two are all manner of possibilities."

"Such as?"

"There are many ways human beings adapt to a situation. Paranoia, hallucination, passive aggression, hypochondria, fantasy, repression, humour, planning, and denial are a few. People use them all trying to return to their happy point. The key is to choose the healthy adaptation to any problem."

'Yes," I said. "But your denial did not solve your problem. Instead, it seems like it solved a problem for your friend."

"Yes, I lost my husband but my loss was due to flapping gums, not denial."

"All right," I said. "Based on that, how would *you* evaluate your life? Would you say that, overall, you've been happy, my immature malcontent?"

Adriana waved her finger at me. "If you recall, I asked you first," she said. "But I'll answer anyway."

"Of course you will, but before you do . . . you must realize that your question is foolish — like asking someone if they are well-fed, or if they have a satisfying sex life. Queries of that nature are always answered in the moment, but they make sense only when viewed through the filter of time. During a life one will be satiated and go hungry many times, just as one's sex life will vary from wild pleasure to extreme disappointment. The highs and lows must be averaged to determine the answer to your question."

"Explain yourself, old man."

"For example, if I haven't eaten since yesterday I won't think I'm well fed, and if I've just recovered from an earthquake-like erotic encounter then I will answer yes, I do have an incredible sex life, even though that might be the only libidinous experience I've had in years. So the answers can be deeply misleading and the question, *are you happy?* can be the most misleading of all. Do you understand?"

"Of course I understand. We must look at our whole résumé. A snapshot at any point can be wrong. The reason I asked is that you and I can look back at almost an entire life to make our assessments. The question of happiness is meaningless when put to a young person. I admit that the answers make more sense as we age, but only if we have enough sense to consider our entire span. Eighty years of experience is more meaningful than three years of angst."

I had her and I pounced. "But that's theory, my puerile prognosticator. In reality happiness does not always dwell in old age because some tend to become unhappy as they contemplate more limited capabilities."

"That has nothing to do with it," she said. "When I recall the highs and lows of my life, it is clear that happiness is somehow tied to human relationships. The times when I have been most happy or unhappy have been as a result of my relationships with those who are closest to me. I think the key is not in how well-fed we are or how often we reached orgasm last Tuesday, but whether or not we have personal relationships that are satisfying, close and meaningful. It matters little with whom we entwine our lives — a lover, a sibling, a parent, or a friend. The point is that for happiness to exist, our lives *must* be entwined. In other words, our degree of happiness corresponds directly to the degree that we have achieved intimacy in our personal lives."

She smiled and we both lapsed into silence. I noticed my heart beating in an irregular way and the patio seemed to light up, making the sky flat and dark. Brambly shadows darted forward and licked my feet. I felt a weird expectancy but the silence became awkward and I left for home. Later, I thought of our conversation and it occurred to me that my life was richer and I was happier since Adriana had moved next door. At times, I even found her insults a satisfying alternative to the emptiness that would exist were she not my neighbour.

A Lazy Busboy

ADRIANA'S STORY ABOUT THE HUSBAND WHO demonstrated little skill in the erotic arts had brought back another memory. Notwithstanding her insults which have no tangible foundation and which owe their genesis to an unspoken acknowledgement that my life has been populated by an assortment of wonderful dalliances while hers has often foundered in the squalls one encounters on the high seas of matrimony, I admit there were times when my confidence trembled and when I contemplated removing myself from active participation in the game of love

I am not an uneducated man and I know that it is possible for the gauge that measures the level in one's testosterone tank to occasionally dip below the warning mark. Just as the best hitter in baseball will occasionally encounter a slump, so too is it possible for one of my skill, intelligence, prowess, drive, and acumen to experience periods of limp performance. My encounter with the sagging phenomena occurred years ago.

Initially, I didn't worry. I have an incredible imagination and memory, and I thought that by enlisting these two helpmates I would quickly solve my problem. Nude waitress at Don Emilio's clad only in black stockings: *nada*. Large breasted neighbour bathing: *nada*. Girls' locker room orgy: *nada*. Couple making love in lighted window: *nada*. My memory and imagination were not the parts on strike.

The lady's name was Monica and she didn't understand that engine failure during the crucial lap on the mattress, like a jockey falling off a horse in the home stretch, is objectively an episode of minor import. However, like a perceived social slight, it may grow into a situation that demands corrective action if only to assuage one or both party's mental uncertainty.

To this end, after I had led my horse to Monica's water trough a number of times without so much as getting it to take a small sip, I decided that if I was ever again to participate in the bedroom sweepstakes, I would have to engage a trainer who not only understood my particular mount but was also familiar with all aspects of the kingly sport.

Accordingly, I made an appointment with Dr. Sofia Olivia Salazar, a renowned psychotherapist and love coach. Known to her patients as Dr. S.O.S., she was famous for charging huge fees for her treatments. She brushed a wandering strand of grey hair away from her eyes and gave me a wide smile as I entered her office. "Welcome. What can I do for you?"

"It's simple," I replied. "My . . . My . . . " I could go no further. I, a man who takes pride in being completely open when it comes to any aspect of love, libido, physicality, or personality, could not speak of my problem, even to this trained professional. "I'm sorry," I said. "I can't go on." I stood and prepared to leave.

"Don't go," she said. "I've encountered this reticence many times. There's a simple solution. Sit down."

I did as she asked and watched as she removed a large pendant that hung around her neck. Then she stood, came around her desk and stopped in front of me. "Stare at the pendant and concentrate on my voice," she said. The golden orb dispersed flashes of light as she swung it back and forth in front of my face. In a low soothing voice she began to chant,

Do not fear what might transpire,
I'm the best that you could hire.
Do now tell what your visit means,
It's now or never, spill the beans.

I felt myself becoming sleepy. Slowly her voice receded until it seemed to come from a great distance. "Now explain your problem," she commanded. "Why have you come to see me?"

I was suddenly charged with a great amount of courage. "It's this way," I explained. "My mental blueprint for love is un-smudged and therefore it is legible, but I am having difficulty turning the two dimensional plan into a multi-dimensional experience."

Dr. S.O.S. snapped her fingers and I awoke instantly. "It's remarkable," I exclaimed. "You induced my brain to function, unhindered by embarrassment or fear."

She nodded. "You suffer from a common affliction. During arousal and its aftermath, it's normal for a man's brain to go to sleep while the critical part of his anatomy springs into an alert state. Your condition occurs when the body mixes up the signals causing your brain to stay alert while the other part begins to snore. Your brain becomes agitated when it is unable to convince your slumbering busboy to become master of ceremonies. Treatment is easy — reverse the signals. You must come to my office every week for therapy. Eventually we will trick your body into rerouting the messages."

"How long will this treatment take?"

"It depends. It could be lengthy if the situation is entrenched."

"And what will it cost?"

"Again that depends. My skill is not inexpensive."

"Isn't there some way we can shorten the duration and lower the cost?"

"There is," she admitted. "But I am hesitant to use it. I can teach you self-hypnosis. You will have to do exactly as I instruct."

"I promise. Let's try it."

"Very well. I will plant a hypnotic suggestion in your brain using a mantra that, when quoted, will immediately activate the behaviour in the suggestion." She snapped her fingers and instantly her voice again came from far away. "The mantra is to be recited only when faced with a critical bedroom situation. You are not to use it at any other time. I'll make an appointment for you to see me in one month so that we can discuss your progress. Now follow the instructions in this ditty:

Remember later what I've said,
Put the thinking part to bed.
Release this body from its strife,
Make the flounder full of life."

She snapped her fingers. "Your appointment is over," she said as she relieved my wallet of its contents. "Remember, when faced with your dilemma, simply repeat the phrases. Your problem will disappear as quickly as a sailor's money in a cathouse. Now go home and enjoy the rest of your life."

My feet barely touched the ground as I left the doctor's office. I hurried straight to Monica's to share the good news.

Adriana and I were enjoying a late evening libation. My glass was almost empty and I was aware that she had been itching to obstruct my story. I paused and poured each of us a fresh brandy.

"Before you go on," she said, "it is my opinion that you were misdiagnosed. I don't believe there was a mix-up in the signals.

Judging by what I already know, I doubt that there was ever a time when your brain was alert."

I returned to my chair.

"Tell me," she said, "Did the treatment work? It must have taken forever. Trying to repair any of your maladies would be like trying to restore the walls at Jericho."

I waited for silence. "You're partly right, my mesmerizing madwoman. The treatment was less than successful. It didn't work at all. A month later, seated in the doctor's office, I was a very dispirited man."

❧

"Welcome back," Dr. S.O.S. said. "Have you won your battle? Is your love life improved? Have you recovered your upstanding ability?"

"No, no, and no! If anything it's worse. I still have the same affliction and now Monica thinks it's permanent."

"Tell me," she said.

"I've tried your prescription. It doesn't work. I'm in the same situation as the last time we spoke."

"You must explain," she said.

"When I'm with Monica, everything progresses as it should until the critical point. Not once has your treatment been successful."

The doctor looked puzzled. "I don't understand," she said. "It's worked in one-hundred percent of similar situations. Tell me exactly what you're doing."

"I'm following your instructions."

She pushed a pad and pencil across her desk. "Write out the mantra for me."

"Very well, but I feel foolish." I took the pencil and wrote, *Remember later what I've said,*

Put the thinking part to bed.
Release this body from its strife,
Make the flounder full of life.

She looked at the pad. "You have it correct. I don't understand. Is there anything you're not telling me?"

"No, I just do what you instructed."

"Tell me exactly what you do."

"I recite your poem."

"Anything else?"

"I don't have a pendant so I usually use a substitute."

"A substitute! What kind of substitute?"

"Whatever is handy. Often I use my pocket watch. Last night I couldn't find it so I used a string of frankfurters from the ice box."

"That must have been difficult — waving frankfurters in front of your eyes and repeating the mantra at the same time."

"Eyes! I didn't wave them in front of my eyes! You swung the pendant where it was needed — in front of my mouth when I couldn't speak. So, I did what you did. I dangled them where they were needed . . . where I dangle."

Dr. S.O.S. raised her eyebrows. "No wonder you still have a problem. You're not to wave anything. I used a pendant only to hypnotize you that first time . . . when I gave you a trigger that would work post-hypnotically."

"So why doesn't it work?" I asked.

"I think that I misdiagnosed you. My prescription was wrong. It says to put your thinking part to bed, but I'll wager that near the crucial moment you are doing all of your thinking with the lower part of your anatomy. Then it tells you to make your limp one full of life. Again it was wrong. Your brain was limp and the mantra woke it up."

"I don't understand," I said.

"Don't you see? Both of your parts were asleep and we woke the wrong one. I believe this to be the case because no one with an alert brain would wave frankfurters in front of his genitals. You were using a prop that you didn't need and repeating a mantra not made for your condition. What we must do is wake up the correct organ. I'll give you a new poem."

She then recited,

"Do not question when or why,
Sing the brain a lullaby.
Know this task will not take long,
Let the organ play its song."

She leaned back and smiled. "Repeat this and all should be well. Your lazy busboy may not become master of ceremonies, but he will get back to work."

Adriana was grinning. "So, did it work? Did your busboy cross the picket line? Was Monica pleased with the results?"

"One question at a time. Yes it worked. Although he has suffered frequent unemployment, my busboy has not gone on strike for years. Unfortunately, Monica left — she suffered from a lack of self-esteem and didn't think herself worthy of me."

"Not worthy of *you*. I don't believe it."

"Believe it . . . she said she couldn't live with my everlasting importance."

"I too knew Monica," Adriana crowed. "She told everyone in town that she had to leave because of your everlasting *impotence*. But, I know the lesson in the story."

"What's that, lumpkin?"

"Reciting poetry while waving one's wiener is not a sound prescription for an evening of love."

A Sexual Primer

DURING MY LONG LIFE I HAVE undertaken many expeditions to explore the outermost regions in the kingdom of love. It occurs to me that I would be doing you, the reader, a serious disservice were I not to provide you with explicit descriptions of the acts committed by those individuals who are sexually affiliated, each with the other, and that I would be remiss were I not to also provide you with step-by-step instructions on how to perform the described acts. To carry out this task it will be necessary to enumerate the variety of fleshly combinations extant in today's world and to exposit the essential qualities of each.

Relationships of a sexual nature occur in a variety of forms. They can be between a man and a woman, between a man and a man, between a woman and a woman, between many people and many other people, between individuals and inanimate objects, and between various parts of one's own anatomy. In addition there are numerous permutations including a *ménage à trois*, a *ménage à quatre*, a *ménage à cinq* and others, ranging to whatever sized *ménage* can comfortably fit in a double bed.

Because of the abundance of possibilities it is necessary to limit the number of arrangements that I will include. Except for occasional comment, I will concentrate my attention exclusively to acts that are performed one-on-one by the male and female genders. To be considered eligible for inclusion, a particular sex act must occur between a man and a woman on the same day and in roughly the same location. Start and end times should be approximately the same for both parties to ensure the duration for each is more or less equal. For example, if a man begins a sex act at 9:00 PM and finishes at 9:03 PM, giving an elapsed time of three minutes, then ideally the act should also take three minutes for the woman. There are four possible outcomes if these conditions are not met:

Man starts first, finishes first. This means, of course, that the woman starts last and never catches up. Although it is considered bad form for the man to begin first, it is not illegal. It is inappropriate, however, for him to begin before the woman is present, and it is considered the ultimate faux pas for him to both start *and* finish before she arrives on the scene. The sequence of events is predictable. When done, the man rolls over and begins to snore, provoking the woman into the realization that she has been left to her own devices. Rather than take the road less travelled, she often abandons the entire activity and begins to hum the music to "Is That All There Is?", whereupon the man wakens and inaugurates a question and answer session concerning last year's World Series. The disparity of results means that this play closes on opening night precluding any chance of a second performance. In ancient Vedic texts this event is referred to as *The Dash of the Rabbit*.

Man starts first, finishes second. Here, the woman ends first — an inadvisable outcome as research has shown that, in this situation, females tend to become bored and will wander away to engage in some other activity such as origami or tree planting. Occasionally, she may begin another sex act but it is rarely with the same man. Some males have suggested that women suffer from a short attention span but this comment is churlish and usually made in a fit of pique. In ancient Vedic texts this event is referred to as *The Ascent of the Tortoise*.

Man starts second, finishes first. While technically a different outcome, the fact that the man finishes first means that all of the details of Event #1 apply, although because he has acted in a gentlemanly fashion and allowed his partner to spring first from the starting gate, he accumulates goodwill — goodwill to the extent that the woman may refrain from humming, "Is That All There Is?" and replace it with the refrain from "Speedy Gonzalez". This outcome is referred to in ancient Vedic texts as *The Rerun of the Rabbit*.

Man starts second, finishes second. Like her opposite in Event #1, the woman should refrain from beginning the sex act before the arrival of her partner, although a woman starting early has been known to act as a powerful motivator for the man. This event is so rare that it is not mentioned in ancient texts but has been referred to in professional circles as *Ice Forming in Hades*.

The sex act, like a written story, should contain a beginning, a middle, and an end. It is assumed that prior to commencing sexual activity one has already met the partner of his or her dreams and has entered the seduction stage. During this phase both individuals should come to the realization that a liaison, if not mutually beneficial, might at least be pleasurable. Then the moods of both parties should be brought into alignment so that an agreement is possible on a sexual course of action. The female mood can be swung to the appropriate angle by the male, engendering sympathy — often accomplished by lingering over a candle-lit dinner while he describes the excruciating loss of a dearly-loved childhood pet. When required, the sympathy index may be increased by the simple act of shedding a tear. If this proves difficult, the man can sometimes persuade a teardrop to appear by surreptitiously plucking a nose hair at the precise moment Old Shep draws his final breath.

The female is most likely to manufacture a proper mood in the male by increasing his testosterone level. This can be accomplished by asking him to repeat, a minimum of three times, the incredible story of how, against all odds, he scored the winning touchdown in the very first Super Bowl played within the confines of his former high school. In the unlikely event that he is not a football hero, simply ask him to recount the bravest thing he's ever done. The woman should be sure she is comfortable because neither tale is a short story.

Just as a novel needs a strong beginning to captivate the reader, so too should the sex act begin with an activity that engages at least one of the participants. Unlike the novel, however, it is not advisable to initiate action too quickly. Things must proceed logically and in the correct order. No one would believe fiction where a character uttered unnatural dialogue. Not so in the sex act. Here it matters little whether the dialogue is believable or not. What is important is that discourse fit with the partner's erotic fantasies. For example, if a woman is turned on by dreams of spending a lazy afternoon in the arms of Hollywood's leading man, then it is imperative that the man not whisper details of his reveries concerning whipped cream and baloney sandwiches.

Once each party, either verbally or internally, has propelled his or her imagination off the runway, the middle of the episode has truly been achieved. Just as a well-constructed tale should contain nothing that does not relate directly to the story, a well-constructed sexual act should contain little that detracts from the performance. An extraneous character should never enter a story simply for the purpose of telling the author's favourite joke. Just so, as the sexual act is progressing, it is not correct for a man to bring up the fact that a previous lover wore transparent underwear, or for a woman to reveal that she can become aroused only by witnessing potential lovers skydiving in the nude. Writer's block may occasionally bring a promising novel to a premature end. So too with love — shovelling inappropriate verbal fuel may cause blockages that makes the sex train lose steam and chug to an early conclusion — a phenomenon known as *evaporating mood* which usually receives no higher than a D-minus when sexual acts are graded.

In the realm of literary fiction, it is important that there not be separate climaxes for each character in a story. In the sexual narrative it is not only acceptable but *de rigueur* that each character reach his or her own specific climax although, as already mentioned, they should occur as near to one another as possible, both physically and chronologically. When that occurs, it may be said that the sex train has truly reached its terminal destination and preparations can then be undertaken for the return journey.

When I informed Adriana of my prescriptions, she shook her head, cleared her throat and said, "Like every meal you prepare, the entree is missing from the menu. Do you not know that there are more facets to love than speed, time, and location?"

"What facets?"

"Group factors, for one."

"Group factors! I'm not talking about *that* type of sex."

"I know, but the world's population has skyrocketed."

"So?"

"The more people in the world, the more they tend to form groups and subgroups."

"You mean, cultures?"

"Not quite. Think about it. It used to be that sex was problematic only when moving outside one's culture or one's age bracket or one's geographic area. Now things are more complicated."

"Enlighten me, my gargantuan groupie."

"Think of all the different groups of people in the world that cut across cultural, age, and geographic boundaries."

"You mean groups like athletes or librarians?"

"Now you're getting it," she said. "The list is unlimited. Apart from obvious categories like librarians, mechanics, or teachers, there are hundreds of lesser known subgroups."

"Such as?"

For example, one group might be Men Who Hate Yogurt . . . and a subgroup is Men Who Hate Yogurt But Eat It to Please Their Wives."

"You're rubbing my leg."

"No, there are thousands: Steer Wrestlers Who Mumble While Gardening; Women Who Laugh Heartily at Unfunny Jokes Told by Dwarfs; Men with Big Egos and Small Tattoos; Bus Drivers Who Pick Their Noses at Red Lights; People Who Surreptitiously Pass Wind while Coughing; Men Who Write Their Names when Urinating on Snow."

"What is your point, woman who drinks brandy and spouts gibberish."

"The point, my simple sex sage, is that problems may arise when members of one group attempt to have a relationship with members of another group."

"An example . . . I need an example."

"How about when someone from the group Men Who Love Mud Wrestling, meets a woman from the group Ladies Who Wear Gloves to Open Doors."

"I see what you mean. That *would* be a problem."

" . . . and Men Who Spit While Talking do poorly courting Women Who Sidestep Slowly."

She was wound up and I decided to play along. "How about, Men Who Refuse to Clean Up After Dogs will get nowhere with Women Who Walk Barefoot in the Park."

"Now you understand," she said. "Some of the problems are so pervasive that the acts that cause them have been given names."

'Go on."

"Take, for instance, the case of a lady from the group Woman Who Relish Unconventional Sex. When she engages with a man who stores his adventure gene under his mattress — say someone from the group Men Who Colour Inside The Lines, or perhaps from the group Men Who Stuff Their Own Shirts, the act has come to be known as, *what in hell are you doing?* The onset of this interaction and its cessation are almost simultaneous."

"You're right. I haven't dealt with group factors and you've raised other issues that I've neglected."

Now *she* was puzzled. "What issues?"

"You mentioned that the world's population has skyrocketed. That means there's a mathematical issue."

"Explain yourself, my numerical nincompoop."

"It's simple. The more people there are, the more sex occurs."

"How is that an issue — apart from more groups?"

'Don't you see? It's like soccer . . . or anything else. The more there is, the more the overall quality improves . . . and the more the quality improves, the greater the chance that records will be set and broken."

"So what?" she asked.

"Whenever there is a chance to break records, competition increases . . . and the more competition, the more rigorous the training. It brings up the whole issue of competitive sex."

"There's no such thing."

"Yes, there is. It's already started. The writing is on the wall."

"Now you're rubbing my leg."

No, I'm not. New industries have developed to complement the onset of tournaments in the realm of physical love."

"Name one," she demanded.

"Okay. Do you honestly think that sports drinks were created to increase stamina at lawn bowling tournaments? No! Their real function is to replace electrolytes lost during intense sexual activity. Entire manufacturing enterprises have entered the field. Less than one year ago a team led by Professor Dimitri Flaboff at the University of Vladivostok invented a machine he called the SX-6-9-9, but it had to be scrapped after it was used by two researchers to smash the world record for number of orgasms per hour."

'Why? Why was it scrapped?"

"The researchers never recovered. The woman, a Ph.D. candidate in microbiology, is now barely able to hold a job slinging hamburgers at McDonald's. The man, a post-doctoral linguistics expert, now has difficulty putting three words together."

'That's terrible," she said.

"Another factor is nutrition. Unfortunately, competitive sex has spurred the creation of special diets."

"Why do you say unfortunately?"

"The diets pose a danger to the continuing existence of some species."

'What danger?"

"There's already a worldwide shortage of rhinoceros horn and, by next year, oysters will be on the endangered list."

"That's also terrible."

"Yes it is, but the biggest problem has been totally hushed up and is almost unknown by the general public."

"What's that?" she asked.

"The entrance of steroids and other performance enhancing drugs into the field. No one knows how many of today's star performers are actually doping, but close observers believe that it's common."

"Can't they test?"

"Yes, but testing has proven to be useless. Participants have discovered that taking a legal impotence drug will mask the use of a banned substance. It's like building a high-rise in front of a bookie joint. The huge erection obscures the illegal activity. Unfortunately, competition is so fierce that athletes will abuse anything that modern science puts in front of them, and there are always coaches who bend all rules in search of instant glory."

"Is it that pervasive?" she asked.

"Not completely. There are still places where traditional sex is practiced and probably will continue to be. But as world population grows and as the number of matches increases, we can expect the worst out of human nature."

"What *does* the future hold?"

"There is a movement to make sex an Olympic event."

"The *Olympics.* Now you are kidding."

"No, I'm not. And due to the nature of the sport it will probably be the first event to be held at both summer and winter Olympiads."

"I understand," she said. "It's a year-round activity in all countries. You've certainly provided an eye opener, my effete athlete."

"It is an eye opener. My only regret is that I was born late. Given my background and experience I would have stood on the podium numerous times."

Adriana stood to go to the bathroom. "Either that or you would have been disqualified for jumping off the starting block before the pistol was fired."

I was left in welcome silence. It occurred to me that she had again succeeded in derailing my communication with you, dear reader. I have not completed the task I had set for myself which was to inform you of the various permutations and combinations that men and women arrive at when cohabiting each with the other. I will not attempt completion of that portion of my project — those who so desire may anticipate the outcome by closely examining Dante's description of the inferno. Instead I will perform a greater service by making the reader aware of the types of men and women one encounters in this world and to provide guidelines so that each type may be identified before one prematurely commits oneself. I will also detail the actions required to deal in an appropriate manner with each identified type.

Deadbeats, Philanderers, and Lowlifes

As PROMISED, I WILL NOW DIVIDE the two genders into their various types and provide guidelines for strategies to be employed when courting a representative of any particular one. I do this because there are thousands of Adriana's groups and no one person embodies the full repertoire of behaviours needed to make him or her attractive to another in any specific typology. I will, of necessity, paint with a wide brush when I sort men and women into their recognizable categories.

To begin, women must understand that there are only two types of men: those who can be changed or made-over and those who, despite all efforts, defy any attempt at alteration. Let's deal first with men who can be changed. There are two of them. They are named Lyle and they live near each other in a remote farming village southwest of Bucharest. Both are committed bachelors.

The second category is, men who can't be changed. This group is comprised of all males other than the two Lyles and is made up of three recognizable subcategories: deadbeats, philanderers, and lowlifes.

1. The Deadbeat: This type of man comes in many guises. He may be a lunkhead, a charmer, a layabout, or a wheedler. To maintain

NEIL McKINNON

his lifestyle, a deadbeat may employ some of the methods used by the philanderer such as flattery, charm, soft-soap, and apple-polishing although often his attempts to use these sophisticated methodologies are amateurish and ham-fisted. Women must exercise caution because, once the deadbeat is attached, cutting him loose can be as difficult as trying to disengage from one's own shadow.

The deadbeat frequently hitches himself to women who are unable to grasp life by the chest hair. One such woman was Adele M. She spent years fluttering in and out of her own emotional purgatory, never focusing on her true talent, which was her ability to clear a room by answering the question, how are you? Stumbling through life's brambles, her eyes firmly fixed on her shoes, she had no idea that Leonard, the sprightly gentleman who, one day, appeared next to her claiming to be an unemployed orthodontist was, in reality, a well practiced deadbeat. He used all of the stock tricks and gradually, as slowly and unobtrusively as lint enters a belly button, he inserted himself into her life.

Adele and Leonard were soon married and presented to the world a picture of bliss, a picture as contrived as any image created by a photographer's trick lens. The maddening thing is that Adele is unaware of Leonard's deadbeat status and, though he hasn't peered inside a mouth for years, she frequently introduces him as "my husband, the doctor." The sad thing is that as long as she continues to provide Leonard with shelter, food, drink, and money, he will be quite willing to play the role of the contented husband . . . but should Adele lose her job as an in-store counsellor to born-again sales clerks, or should she come on hard times for any other reason, Leonard will disappear from her life as quietly and quickly as flatulence vanishes on a windy day.

What Adele does not know is that there is a foolproof method to identify a deadbeat. Early in the relationship she should simply have asked Leonard for a loan. A true deadbeat responds to a loan request in one of two ways. He either vanishes into thin air never to be seen again, or he asks the woman for her dead mother's wedding ring in order that he might pawn it and lend her the money. In the first instance, the woman should hold on to her skirts as the whirlwind caused by the rapidity of the deadbeat's departure is truly mind boggling. In the second, the woman should take her mother's wedding ring, pawn it herself and go on an extended holiday to a remote beach. She should remain there until the deadbeat himself solves the problem by turning his attention to greener and more lucrative pastures.

2. The Philanderer: This gentleman is immediately identified by his unique odour, an enticing mixture of after-shave and grease tainted by a faint whiff of the psychological glue that he uses to stick himself to unsuspecting women, much like summer bluebottles attach themselves to flypaper. He has been in and out of more relationships than Lothario, Casanova, and Don Juan combined.

In the beginning the philanderer is considerate and accommodating. He basks in the lady's beauty. He revels in her conversation. But all the time his eyes are peering in two directions: back at the procession of devastated women disappearing into the horizon, and forward to the future as he sniffs out his next dalliance.

The reason he's enthralled with anyone is that he's enthralled with everybody. He's a loving lunatic — a horndog. His stamina is amazing. He can't stay away. He's here. He's there. No, he's back here. He's everywhere. He's ready to go again . . . and again . . . and again. He is an addict of indiscriminate lubricity, routinely unfaithful to his wife, his girlfriends, his wife's friends, and his friends' wives. His horizons have expanded exponentially, from high school where he nursed an intense desire to nuzzle every girl in his graduating class, to university where his aspirations grew to encompass all of the women in the faculty where he studied physical education. Eventually, his ambition knew so few bounds that he secretly craved to bed the entire female population of a state or province. He is an expert at bedroom multitasking and is restricted by few technical limitations.

The philanderer never takes time off and has never had a real holiday. His work, his recreation, his avocation and his hobby are the chase. The only time he has been known to relax is during career day at the local high school where he fondly recounts how he became successful in his chosen profession.

For an example of the havoc wreaked by the philanderer we need look no further than the tragic story of Sarah B., a deeply religious girl who thought her chance meeting and subsequent affair with Desmond, a sometime ski instructor and sweet-talking alley cat, was her ticket away from her stuffy liberal parents who did not subscribe to her right-wing religious philosophy and who constantly encouraged her to lighten up.

Sarah met Desmond at a fundamentalist revival meeting where she had gone to seek solace after her parents had presented her with a membership in a radical animal rights group as a gift for her twenty-first birthday. Desmond had attended the revival because long ago he had discovered that at this venue, dressed in a beard, sandals and flowing robe, seducing young women became as easy as ushering lambs to slaughter. Using equal amounts of sweet-talk, charm, flattery, and sympathy, as well as dashes of piety, sprinklings of biblical quotations and small chunks of prayer, Desmond penetrated Sarah's awareness, entered her consciousness, broke through her perimeter, infiltrated her defences, inserted himself into her heart and finally, in what was his best time yet, he squirrelled his way into her pants.

At first Sarah felt guilty because she had broken a promise she had made to herself years before: to preserve all alterable pieces of her anatomy in a pristine state until her wedding night, or until judgement day, whichever came first. But glib, sweet-talking Desmond soon convinced her that what they were doing — by then almost on an hourly basis — was, in reality, responding to a higher power. Once he had explained this, Sarah recognized their indiscretions as simple peccadilloes and soon she was able to immerse herself in trying to satisfy the quirky shifts in Desmond's bedroom behaviour, shifts she soon came to enjoy. After all, he looked exactly like a picture of Jesus and she knew that the whole sordid affair would drive her atheist parents crazy.

All this might have worked out if Desmond had not been a philanderer. However, monogamy is as foreign to philanderers as pork is to rabbis so, of course, he could not stay. The philanderer is trapped by his libertine nature. He must change partners as often as Prometheus changed livers . . . and so it was that Sarah awoke one morning to find a note on the pillow where Desmond's head should have been. The note explained that he had finally identified a place in the world, near barren of population but with just enough females of indiscriminate nature, that he felt there was a reasonable chance that he could fulfill his secret ambition. To that end, he was leaving immediately for Saskatchewan.

Sarah was devastated but admitted to herself that it might be for the better. After all, the Lord does move in mysterious ways. The experience has made her more worldly. Nowadays, she quickly exits from the company of any man who gets a wistful look in his eye whenever someone mentions Regina.

3. The Lowlife: I have left the lowlife until last because that is where he must be placed on any measure of human personality, capability, or intelligence. His only skill is the ability to transform oxygen into carbon-dioxide. Because of his limitations, it is impossible for him to raise his status in society. Therefore, as he sees it, he has no choice. Wallowing in despicability, his only goal in life is to attach himself to a woman and, by the sheer weight of his own wretchedness, drag her to a level such that there will be at least one person in the world with less social rank than he.

The lowlife has many aliases. He may be a son of a bitch, a bastard, a heel, a rat-bag, a sleaze-bucket, or a no-goodnik. It is impossible for him to have an inferiority complex as he really is inferior. The lowlife can be identified in two ways: First, by his location. He is always either in or near a bar. Second, unlike the deadbeat or the philanderer, he does not charm or flatter. In one sense he is more honest than they, in that he does not pretend to be someone other than who he is, a no-class worm. He also does not pretend that he will change. Actually, he expects the woman to change. To this end he employs all sorts of tricks and is not above subterfuge . . . or below it, for that matter.

One example should suffice — the sad tale of Maria M. and a lowlife named Geraldo. Maria was a naive girl, the illegitimate daughter of an itinerant hairdresser — a woman with no permanent clientele — and a one-time Baptist preacher turned shoemaker, a man who had gone from saving souls to replacing them. Maria had never learned that there's a difference between hugging and being held so you can't get away. One fateful day, she stopped for a drink on her way home from her job as an assistant message taker at a beef jerky factory. Geraldo, who sported greasy hair and crooked teeth was, as usual, patrolling the bar in search of prey. He approached Maria and said, "Haven't I seen you someplace before . . . and would you like to come back to my place?"

It was at this point that Maria made her mistake. Had she recognized Geraldo for the lowlife that he was and had she countered with an appropriate response, much of what followed might have been avoided. An appropriate response in the foregoing situation would have been, "Yes we have met. I'm the receptionist at the VD clinic." Or, "Back to your place, you say. Can two people fit under a rock?"

Instead, Maria, who was not wise to the ways of the lowlife, responded. "Maybe we've met . . . do you eat beef jerky?"

Her reply was too mild and Geraldo interpreted it as an invitation, not that he needed one. She didn't stand a chance. He was all over her like goose crap on a beach. They returned to his place and within a week he had diluted her self-esteem to the point where she believed that she owed him everything and had to complete her life with him in order to repay. After all, it was her fault that he had crooked teeth — if he hadn't bought her drinks on the night they met, he would have been able to afford a trip to the orthodontist.

Scum like Geraldo can always be identified by his opening lines when he encounters a potential victim. In order to provide armour for unsuspecting females, I reproduce here, a few of the more common introductions employed by this brand of sub-human, and the proper response to ensure that play in this game is suspended in the first inning:

Lowlife: "I want to give myself to you."

Woman's Proper Response: "Sorry, but I already have a pet snake."

Lowlife: "I've wanted to go out with you ever since I read all that stuff on the bathroom wall."

Woman's Proper Response: "Love to, but tonight I'm attending the opening of my garage door."

Lowlife: "If I could rearrange the alphabet, I'd put U and I together."

Woman's Proper Response: "If I could rearrange it, I'd put F and U together."

Lowlife: "So, what do you do for a living?"

Woman's Proper Response: "I'm a female impersonator."

Lowlife: "If you were a book, I'd crawl between your covers."

Woman's Proper Response: "A book! You probably think Peter Pan is something to put under the bed and that Moby Dick is a venereal disease."

Lowlife: "Here I am. What are your other two wishes?"

Woman's Proper Response: "First, that you slither back into your bottle and second, that you put a cork in it."

❧

We were on my patio and Adriana, who had thus far managed to restrain herself, finally lost her battle. "There are many kinds of men you haven't mentioned," she said. "What about stumblebums, dumbos, horses arses, con men, bozos, knuckleheads, letches, blowhards, gasbags and good-time Charleys?"

"Your list is long, my loquacious lumpkin, but the terms on it are all synonyms for, or subcategories of, the types I have already dealt with."

'I see," she said. "Then there are no others?"

"No, my list covers them all."

"Into which category do you fit?" she asked. "No, let me guess. My first thought is that you are a deadbeat because you don't work and the fact that you are lazy lends weight. But then, though you lack skill in the bedroom and though you have never visited Saskatchewan, you also fit the profile of a philanderer. That left me perplexed as you practically live in a bar and you have ensnared women in that environment although, to my knowledge, all came to their senses and quickly left. So I conclude, my mistyped tyro, that you are all of the above." Over the rim of her glass, she gave me a look, similar to the smirk a cat exhibits when the door is left open on a birdcage.

I returned her grin. "You have me there."

"I thought so," she purred. "Your categories are useless. There is some of each in all men."

"You're right . . . except for one thing . . . my middle name is Lyle."

She grinned and saluted me with her glass. "Slippery," she said, "very slippery. But weren't you about to detail the different types of women in the world?"

My glass was empty and I was weary. "Another time . . . categorizing women is not an easy task. Even someone as experienced as I will occasionally make a mistake."

A Morning Walk

A RISING SUN CHASED THE SCENT OF oleander through my open window and together they nudged me into awareness that this was no ordinary morning. A glance outside confirmed it. The understated beauty of daybreak cast reflections of the surrounding mountains onto Lake Albatross and a misty horizon softened the worn peaks so that they looked like the flattened breasts of a reclining woman. I called through the window to Adriana who was harassing the flowers in her garden and we agreed to walk to Don Emilio's so that she could buy me breakfast.

As we started down the hill, the sun topped the horizon and turned the approaching pavement to silver. The *carretera* had been noticeably washed clean by the rainy season and was lined with bouquets of orange-red flowers lifted into the sky by gigantic tulip trees. We decided to multiply the distance by three to prolong our enjoyment.

"It's a gorgeous morning," Adriana said. "Are you going to spoil it by trying to categorize women as you did men — by confining us in your prefabricated boxes?"

"It is not my intention to confine women," I replied. "I simply wish to point out certain types and provide guidelines for men who enter into relationships with those types. Again, it will be necessary to paint with a wide brush. But I do not wish to walk and talk at the same time."

"That is your choice," she said. "Unlike whether or not you simultaneously breathe and think."

Before I go on, dear reader, I must explain that the Principality of Adriana alternates between two states: natural bland and tippled fishwife. Prior to breakfast her demeanour leans away from natural bland.

We walked randomly for over an hour, passing the doors of any number of strange buildings, each of which displayed a darkened interior and CLOSED signs in their windows. Eventually the delicious smells of early morning cooking led us to Don Emilio's. Remembering the season, we chose to sit under a tiled roof and look out to the open courtyard. At this hour we were the only customers — *huevos rancheros* and steaming coffee arrived almost immediately.

I tugged a paper napkin from a ceramic tomato and Adriana spooned sugar from a bowl that came from the same batch. "Go ahead," she said. "Let me hear it."

"Very well . . . there are two basic types of women — those who have it and those who don't. Those who have it make sure it's visible and show it off at every occasion. Those who don't have it envy the ones who do, so they often try to fake it or hide the fact by talking about how useless it is or why it's not needed. They also get angry at a date if he pays attention to someone who has it."

Adriana sipped her coffee. "That's nothing new. Of course, some have ideal bodies and some lack such perfection. If you relied solely on the testimony of women then you have heard that there has never been a female in all of history with a faultless physique. Men are less discriminating. They continually brag of bedding women with consummate physicality." She stood. "I have to go to the bathroom but when I come back I want you to answer a question."

I waved her away and leaned back. A dozen white plastic tables were scattered at random across the courtyard, each surrounded by four chairs tipped forward to shed rain and to expose red and yellow Luna Beer advertisements. Across the courtyard, a stout cook reached through the steam rising from a large pot to turn up the volume on an old radio and mariachi music began to compete with the broadcast of a soccer game coming through the open window from the house across the street.

Adriana returned and sat down. "Now, answer a question, my vacuous voyeur. Explain why males and females look at the same anatomy, yet perceive it differently."

"In a minute, my little suet sack. First I must explain fully the difference between the two types. Those who have it, think men only look at them because of it. Those who don't have it, think that men look at those who do have it for the same reason."

"Yes, yes. Now answer my question. Why *do* men and women see the same body differently?"

"Very well, but I'm not finished. There are many reasons why perceptions vary between the genders, but I'll proffer just one. We all know that women's bodies change through time, but we don't always recognize just how short that time span can be. For example, during the interval that it takes to down several drinks, it is not uncommon for a woman's body to approach absolute flawlessness in the eyes of the man who has consumed the drinks. This same phenomenon has been known to occur to sailors stepping ashore after months at sea.

"Now I'll finish. Those who have it are afraid of losing it while those who don't have it often try to acquire it artificially.

Most of the time, they wish that those who have it would shrivel up or go away. Those who have it, sometimes don't know they have it, and those who don't have it never forget."

We finished our coffee and Adriana paid the cheque. Outside, our city had come alive. A moustached man held a ladder vertical on the street corner and gazed at the sky as if contemplating a climb with no destination. A young mother sputtered by on a motor scooter laughing along with her infant daughter whose chubby legs straddled the gas tank. An old lady sat at a table topped by a green and red umbrella. She was selling all manner of delicious looking things that we had no interest in now that we had eaten. A boy in a yellow t-shirt threw potato chips at his sister while they waited for a bus. A young woman sauntered by, all belly and buttocks, in low-slung jeans. A man with scars on his arms smoked a cigarette and tinkered under the hood of his ancient truck as he furtively watched the undulations in the woman's pants. He caught me staring and we both grinned. Adriana, oblivious to the unspoken lecherous conspiracy, resumed our conversation. "But surely, your so-called phenomenon is explained by the fact that alcohol clouds a man's vision and obviously sea spray does the same thing."

"No, my mangy mariner, I will not enter that debate," I said. "Rather let me finish my exposition of those who have it and those who don't by saying that unfortunately, most men don't have it . . . or at least, not that much of it."

She stared at me. "What are you talking about? I thought we were discussing women's bodies."

"*You* were discussing bodies. *I* was discussing brains. Conversing about a woman's anatomy is for adolescent boys or men with arrested development. Both are like hobbled billy goats sniffing the air for sexual sweat. Sometimes there's a whiff but it goes nowhere. As you say, most women understand that it's impossible to define a perfect body . . . and, may I say it, so do a few sober, land-locked males."

Adriana wrinkled her nose. "Before you go on, my perambulating pontificator, perhaps you can enlighten me as to why many women try to hide their bodies while a man will walk down the street with a bald head, a three-ton stomach, and bowed legs, and still consider himself sexy?"

"That *is* an enigma. Perhaps mirror images cause eye malfunctions in the human male."

On cue, a rotund man in a white hat aimed himself toward the faded white statue of Bartolomé Albatross on the corner of Paseo del Lago. Filled with purpose, he used plenty of space as he walked swiftly trying to undo, in a few minutes on a sidewalk, the years of indulgence at a table. Flowers bloomed in boxes fronting El Castillo de los Tontos, and early morning cooking smells were replaced by the enticing aroma of pies, tarts, cakes, and other dietary unmentionables as we walked past Maria's Bakery.

The aroma captured Adriana and she excused herself to run inside. She emerged in a few minutes carrying *pan dulces* for two. We nibbled on the sweetness as we walked. "I have already detailed the types of men that threaten or destroy a relationship. I will now turn to women. A woman is more complex than a man because, in tandem with the two types, she may fall into dozens of other categories. She may be an aunt or an apron . . . a babe, bimbo, broad, ball-breaker, battle-axe, chick, coquette, daughter, dish, or doll. She might also be a fox, girl, hen, matron, moll, nun, or nympho. If none of the foregoing, she could be a pussy, queen, slattern, sister, slut, shrew, tart, widow, or a wife. The list is not exhaustive and, of course, not all are dangerous. Some that *are* considered menacing, such as prostitutes, hookers, and trollops are really not hazardous. They are simply one half of a transaction — part physical and part financial — that has little consequence in terms of the male-female bond. The real risk to a relationship comes from within. The women that pose the most threat to men are the prospectors, the architects, and the wardens."

A breeze emerged from a side street and I noticed the sky had darkened. At the same time I felt the first drops of the last gasp of the wet season on my face. I shivered and Adriana grinned. "Aren't you cold?" I asked.

"Not at all, my jiggling jellyfish," she said. "I like the cold."

"You should," I replied. "You invented it."

We picked up our pace but in moments the rain clouds melted away to reveal a blue sky.

Let me begin with the prospector. She is an explorer, a searcher, a woman with a quest. Single-mindedly, she pursues her goal — to discover and then mine her own personal male El Dorado.

During the time of human history, since there have been two genders, some women have seen their main function as providing encouragement so that men may quit living lives of unmitigated ease. They deem it an imperative to provide just the right amount of avaricious propellant to nudge any male in their conjugal catchment area into the exalted state of penury. The best known of this classification have been designated trophies, mistresses, and concubines. However, they are nursery rhyme villains compared to the real master of the art — the common housewife.

The housewife operates on many levels. The most obvious and famous are the ones who have married movie or sports stars. Inevitably, citing incompatibility, mental cruelty or some inconsequential peccadillo, they sue for divorce and the gigantic settlement that goes with it. The scenario follows a well known plot, familiar to all. What is not so well known are the activities that never reach the headlines but flourish in the daily lives of ordinary couples, where sex becomes the commodity that is used to bargain for everything from a Caribbean vacation to a new toaster."

As a favour to my male readers I will outline the sad case of Midas Nestfeather who moved here to take his ease beneath our warm sun after acquiring modest wealth in his own country. Midas was a small breezy cog in a research group that had developed a revolutionary process to aid in conservation. After years of experimentation they had succeeded in harnessing the energy potential in human flatulence. The breakthrough had caused an immediate worldwide reduction in electrical consumption and had sent batteries, nuclear power plants, and coal-fired generators into the land of buggy whips and button overshoes. The market reacted wildly. Midas had gotten behind the project early and was there at the tail end. At the peak of the frenzy he sold the few shares he had accumulated, ate his last plate of beans, and retired.

His downfall began shortly after his arrival. He attended a black tie soirée hosted by EBA, the local group established to Elevate Beyond Ability. Membership in this group was restricted to those individuals who demonstrated a rare skill — a skill that, when employed, allowed every member to climb socially over every other member at the same time. Midas's attendance was accidental. He thought EBA stood for Eat Beans Anonymous. When he arrived, the large man employed at the door to keep out riff-raff was distracted by the simultaneous arrival of a pair of large breasts closely followed by a curvaceous lady in a gold lamé dress. Midas entered and found himself alone in a crowd of people all intent on relieving the incredible dreariness, abundant in any echelon that resides at an elevation where lack of oxygen causes synapses to wither. Scattered among these individuals were beautiful women, each raptly feigning attention to every man they systematically sidled past. These women were not members of EBA. They were prospectors, each single-mindedly intent on acquiring mineral rights to any ore-bearing male into whom they could drive a stake. A bystander could have been forgiven for assuming he or she was at a gathering of 49'ers or Klondike sourdoughs. Most of these prospectors were uninvited but had gained entrance by distracting the doorman, usually some days before the soiree.

One such prospector was Belinda Breastwallow — the lady in the gold dress — a beautiful and statuesque redhead prone to spontaneous vivaciousness, but only at appropriate times. Belinda frequently attended these events to explore various shafts in search of outcroppings that she might be able to trace to the main vein. She became excited by her findings when she assayed Midas. Here was gold . . . and possibly a fool, but there was definitely no sign of fool's gold.

Midas was unaware that he was vulnerable. His new aura of wealth rendered him more approachable than had his previous aura. Belinda, for her part, recognized a bonanza. There would be no long days of panning for little gain. His nuggets were exposed for the picking. She could barely resist reaching out to fondle them.

The courtship was swift. Midas never even felt the pick. He fell like a ten pound ingot. In no time at all, Belinda had gathered his nuggets, sluiced his dust, and swallowed his mother lode — all the while fending off any number of claim jumpers. He was soon stripped of every asset and Belinda left to pursue her secret dream, which was to wildcat for oil in the petroleum clubs of Houston, Denver, and Calgary. Midas — broke, broken, and bewildered — moved to the streets. It wasn't long until he fell off the wagon and resumed his gaseous ways. While the prognosis is that he will spend the rest of his days eating in soup kitchens and roaming the alleys of large cities, there is one bright spot. It matters not in what doorway he chooses to sleep, there is zero probability that he will have to share it.

❧

Adriana sighed as I finished. "Very well, metallic mud-brain, but what about housewives? I thought you were going to talk about them."

"Don't you get it, my gilded grump? She and Belinda are sisters. The housewife just operates on a smaller scale and mines at a slower pace. Many can extract ore from the same source for an entire lifetime."

Adriana looked at me as if I had crawled from under the sidewalk. "If I agreed with you we'd both be wrong," she said. "Not all housewives are like that."

"Of course," I agreed. "There are three that are different and they all live southwest of Bucharest."

Our city is home to a host of holidays and fiestas as well as to people who joyfully celebrate every one, so it should be no surprise that church bells tolled and fireworks distracted us as we turned up the dirt path toward the mountains. We climbed far enough so that, when we looked down, we saw red tiled roofs framing egg-shaped cupolas with tiny windows — an appropriate foreground to the green expanse of *lirio* bobbing on a ruffled lake. The city's houses are multi-hued so that a kaleidoscope of changing shapes and colours massaged our eyes as we climbed. We stopped to catch our breath. "Go on," Adriana said. "What about your next group? I believe you said architects."

"Right you are."

❧

Architects are the second group that men should be aware of, although they are harder to spot than prospectors. Rarely does a woman display her architectural credentials until she is married, although long before marriage she will form a mental blueprint of her finished project. They are the least religious of all women as they do not trust God. No matter which of Adam's offspring they set eyes on, all they see are flaws — flaws which they are so sure they can correct that many surreptitiously begin their handiwork on the first date. Most are skilled builders as well as designers. Anticipating a lifetime of work, they begin their reclamation from the ground up or, alternatively, from the outside in.

Altering a male to match one's blueprint is a demanding business. Many architects approach the enterprise as a covert operation. Quietly, they employ a variety of stratagems that are designed to encourage proper behaviour — stratagems that have been termed 'doggy biscuits' as they resemble the reward system used to encourage Fido to roll over or play dead. For example, when training an unenthusiastic man to perform household chores, two of the doggy biscuits that are commonly promised, provided, or withheld are sex and cold beer.

There is no aspect of a male that is beyond an architect's ability to reconstruct: the clothes he wears, the food he eats, his taste in drink, the way he combs his hair. One gentleman of my acquaintance was even spied upon in the bathroom to ensure that he was brushing his teeth in the correct manner. Another, a husband, was corrected by his wife when he mentioned how something he ate had tasted.

❧

Seven times on that short walk someone smiled and wished us good morning. The unkempt goatherd who lives by the path flashed smile number eight and whispered a soft, "*buen dia*." I wished him well and we continued to climb.

❧

For an example of the mangled edifice that may result from an architect's ambition, we need look no further than my old school chum Mario L., a simple and ordinary man except for one aspect — he was a brilliant, if somewhat erratic, archaeologist.

Mario was a chain smoker and prodigious beer drinker who considered himself contented and happy, secure in his pursuit of the artefacts that prehistoric cultures had left behind. He spent entire seasons in little frequented areas of the world, gathering ancient evidence before returning to his laboratory where he solved the riddles of past lifeways. So intent was he on his pursuits that he had allowed some aspects of grooming to wander from his daily itinerary. For example, most of his clothes had holes and he rarely combed his hair or brushed his teeth. He had never entered into an intimate relationship with anyone of either the male or female persuasion and felt no need for the company of either sex. His unencumbered existence suited him fine. That is, it suited him fine until his department head assigned him a graduate student named Delia Alterbody.

Delia really belonged in a different faculty. First and foremost, she was an architect, a project manager, a builder, a changer, and a repairer. Her interest in archaeology was secondary. The moment she saw Mario, she dusted off her mental blueprint and went to work.

❧

"This is interesting," Adriana said. "Do explain."

"All right," I said. "It's not a long story and like all of these projects, it proceeds in three phases: the External, the Domiciliary, and the Internal. First I will discuss the External Phase."

❧

At their very first meeting in Mario's office, Delia wrinkled her nose and asked, "Has someone been eating garlic in here?"

"Why yes," said Mario who had been enjoying a breakfast of strong coffee and garlic sausage in his office for over fifteen years. "Does it bother you?"

"Well, now that you mention it," said Delia. "I do have an allergy to garlic and I prefer tea in the morning." What she neglected to say was that she was allergic to anything she didn't approve of . . . and what Mario soon discovered was that the list of things Delia didn't approve of, although not quite endless, was certainly downwind from infinite.

The thin edge of the wedge proved rather thick, and while it took time for Mario to wean himself from his morning repast, he never again ate it in his office. Less than three weeks and four nose-wrinklings later, a colleague noticed that Mario had also stopped smoking and drinking beer.

A short time later, Delia started on grooming. "You should get the holes mended in the clothes you wear to faculty meetings," she told Mario one day in the graduate students' lounge as he nibbled at the spinach and broccoli quiche she had ordered for his lunch. Mario, while slow in these matters, was not dense. The very next day he appeared in the department wearing a brand new suit. Delia again wrinkled her nose. "Have you been shopping at the Salvation Army store? I know a good tailor and I'd be happy to take you the next time you want to buy clothes. I'm free on Saturday."

Once Delia had completed remaking Mario's physical appearance by having his teeth fixed, by getting his hair cut and showing him how she liked it combed, by insisting he shave every day, by purchasing a new wardrobe and discarding his old one, by having him regularly shine his shoes, and by showing him how to knot the ties she purchased, it was time for the second phase, the Domiciliary.

The seduction was easy. Mario never knew what hit him. He was bedded and wedded before the semester was out. Once Delia moved into his comfortable home, the story sped inevitably toward the foregone conclusion that was to ensure her an exalted place in the annals of female architects everywhere.

Her first order of business was to rearrange the house. This was easy as Mario paid little attention to his surroundings. He spent hours scanning the earth looking for evidence that early people had once trod where he now walked. He hadn't observed anything above ground level for years.

Delia hired an interior decorator who quickly threw out Mario's collection of primitive art and other cultural material. The decorator said it didn't go with the period look she was trying to achieve — early Doukhobour set off by a contemporary Hutterite motif. She also created wall hangings that depicted cartoon characters reciting verses from the Bible. These were hung in Delia's meditation room which had previously functioned as Mario's office. Mario carried his papers to an uncluttered corner of the basement where he was able to work until he was again required to move, this time to the garage as Delia needed the basement space to store the exercise equipment that she had purchased on sale and which she knew they would use someday.

When the house was finished, Delia focused her attention outside. She hired a man to dig up the fruit trees that Mario had nurtured in the backyard, and then she contracted with a firm to construct a swimming pool which she surrounded with marble statues of small, grinning naked boys. The contractor installed a timer and pump so that once every hour the boys, in unison, peed into the pool. She ordered dozens of plastic birds and ceramic dwarfs which she placed strategically, so they were always visible to guests.

Once Delia had completed her home revision she again set to work on Mario. This was the Internal Phase. If they ever intended to start a family he would have to stop all extended absences. The idea of family appealed to Delia and she began to accumulate baby items — a crib, a highchair, and a changing table, which she stored in a corner of the garage. This forced Mario to set up a card table on the sidewalk in order to write his academic papers, although he had limited time to concentrate on research as it took four hours on a bus each day to commute between his home and the university. Delia needed his car to drive the two blocks to her daily exercise class.

Mario's story would be ongoing had it not been for an unfortunate accident. Not being able to do fieldwork severely curtailed his publication of scientific papers and participation in academic conferences. Inevitably, he was passed over in his bid to secure tenure and denied promotion to associate professor. Late one evening, while Delia was asleep, Mario, heartbroken and filled with despair, felt a small knot of rebellion form in his stomach. He fed it a mixture of beer and resentment. Eventually it expanded and rose to the surface of his sagging nature. It bobbed there while he drank more beer. Then he ate a plate of garlic sausage, tore a hole in his new suit, and went outside to smoke a cigarette, leaving the toilet seat up. Clouds covered the moon making it difficult to see. He stumbled into a pink flamingo, took three steps sideways, tripped over a scowling dwarf, and fell into water.

Flailing helplessly and weighted down by twenty pounds of wet, tailor-made wool suit, Mario perished in his own swimming pool. The last faint image he saw before gasping a final breath and sinking to the bottom was that of a grinning boy urinating on him.

🦢

Adriana spoke as we approached her house. "It's a sad tale you spin, but I'm curious as to what became of Delia. Did she suffer remorse? Did she join a convent?"

"No, my marble-faced matriarch. Fate had other plans for her. As she was near completion of her Ph.D., the university held Mario's job open for her and she eventually went on to have a distinguished career, publishing numerous papers based on work that he had done in field seasons prior to their marriage. She was hailed far and wide as a great scholar and quickly filled Mario's well-shined shoes. During her career she married and then redesigned no less than four other members of the department's professorial staff."

Adriana turned into her house and I followed. I noticed that she had a reddened complexion and was breathing faster than she normally does, even when basking in the proximity of my sensuous personality. It was still early but we had walked briskly and a small brandy while sitting in the shade on her patio would serve to slow both of our thumping hearts.

She went inside and returned with a bottle and two glasses. "You mentioned a third type of woman, a warden."

"Yes, I did. Your memory is infallible. Perhaps you have noticed that my three types of women are analogous to the steps taken in the career of any successful tyrant. For example, a dictator acquires all the wealth of his country, builds palaces and monuments to his legacy, and then decides that the way to prevent revolts from the peasantry is to crush them and keep them crushed. It is not unusual for one woman to pass through all three stages in her life. Many, however, are content with typecasting and fill the same role with a succession of partners."

I swallowed my brandy and held out my glass. "The warden is the last of my groupings. She is always in a long-term relationship and has been known by a variety of names through the ages: shrew, nag, fishwife, ogress, harpy, hellcat, and crone are but a few. Just as the architect succeeds the prospector, so the warden succeeds the architect. Barring accidents she will accompany her partner into old age. The warden oversees a jail with one prisoner. Although the crimes vary from marriage to marriage, the punishment is always the same — a life-sentence of hard labour with zero chance of parole. Wardens choose only men whose lack of brains, good looks, or some other important characteristic makes them easy to dismantle and pin down. Their primary objective is control."

Adriana lifted her eyebrows. "Go on . . . given your self-proclaimed wide experience you must have encountered many wardens. Tell me how they affect a man's life."

At this point in my narrative, dear reader, please allow me to speak in a confidential manner. It is my impression that Adriana displays the characteristics of a warden. In the interest of keeping my relationship with her as pleasant as possible, I will construct an example from my imagination. I believe that this will in no way detract from the beneficial nature of my exposition and it will serve to keep Adriana from acquiring the ambition that could make my life a living hell. Bear with me and if she should ask, please vouch for the veracity of my tale. Thank you for your indulgence. With that caveat out of the way, I will now invent a warden who, though she ruins her lover's life, is not successful in her own.

"So you want an example, my crass cupcake. The one that immediately enters my memory is the horrific tale of an artist friend of mine, Pablo T., who had the misfortune to meet and wed a young warden named Graciella just as he was completing art school and about to embark on what should have been a great career."

❧

By the time he graduated, Pablo was already respected in the art community and was on the cusp of becoming known to the world. He was a versatile young man, equally at home in all media. He was also happy, gaining much enjoyment from the time he spent with just his palette for company, and also from helping his fellow students with their projects. There was no question that he had been dealt aces in the game of life.

Graciella met Pablo by chance when she accidentally entered an art gallery that happened to be located next door to the cock fight that she was planning to attend. Pablo was hosting the opening reception for a show of his own work which he had entitled *Angels in a Dull Light,* a series of paintings he had done to illustrate the erotic possibilities of locating the nude female form in bleak landscapes.

He welcomed her at the door. "Come in. Come in. I'm pleased that you could make it. Let me get you a glass of white wine."

"Wine," Graciella said, somewhat bewildered. "I thought the beverage of choice at these events was warm beer. But bring it anyway — white is one of my two favourite kinds."

Pablo returned with the wine and Graciella said, "I'm confused. Where are the cocks?"

"There are no cocks," Pablo replied. "I've painted only women."

They struck up a conversation and Graciella quickly realized her mistake. Pablo fell like a rock in a landslide. In a trance, he abandoned his show and followed Graciella next door. She spent the evening explaining the finer points of the fighting cock and Pablo spent the evening fighting to keep his finer point under control.

They were lovers by morning and were wed within the month. One evening, watching Graciella slide a dress off her rounded body, Pablo observed how the light created and then teased the shadows in all of her nooks and crannies. *My God*, he thought. *She'd make a fantastic model. I have to paint her.*

That night he popped the question, and the next morning Graciella fidgeted, nude on a wooden bench while, across the room, Pablo slapped paint on a large canvas. He worked as if she were the last dream of the night and he only had seconds before waking. In his obsession all previous inspiration meant nothing, no more significant than flowers on wallpaper.

Graciella had never been accused of having an abundance of patience. Sitting for long periods was beyond her capability. She began to take frequent breaks, during which she stood beside Pablo and stared critically at his work. After awhile she commented, "I think my eyes are a deeper shade of blue and my lips are redder than you show them."

When Pablo failed to respond, comment became suggestion. "You should make my cheek bones stand out. Put more colour in them," and "I think you should change the shape of my lips. They're more like petals."

Eventually her mask slipped a bit and suggestion became demand. "You have painted a flaw in my complexion. Take it out now," and "My breasts are fuller than you've shown. I want them redone."

Finally the mask disappeared. Demand changed to criticism. "You don't know what you're doing. How did you ever graduate?" and "I should divide my body and put numbers on it. Then you might make a better likeness."

She grabbed his brush and began to alter everything that he had just painted. Stunned, Pablo staggered over and sat on the bench that she had vacated minutes earlier.

This isn't difficult, she thought. Out loud she said to Pablo, "You stay where you are. *I'm* going to paint *you*." She reached for a fresh canvas.

Pablo, too, had difficulty posing. "Stay still!" Her foot stamped the floor. "If I have to come over there, you'll never move again."

At first Pablo thought she was joking but it became apparent that she took her role as artist very seriously. Though he had been happy in school Pablo was not blessed with a secure nature. In fact it was quite insecure. Soon Graciella was doing all the painting and then she discarded him as a model. He began to run errands for her and when he wasn't so engaged he became a sponge, soaking up tirades as fast as she could deliver them.

When she had completed a number of paintings, Graciella mounted her own exhibition which she titled *Fighting Cock to Fried Chicken: A Retrospective*. Most of her work was inspired by the current relationship and did not impress the critics. One even referred to her painting of a nude Pablo as flaccid. Unfortunately, the negative response was harder on Pablo than it was on Graciella. Rejection passed straight through her, pausing only long enough to pick up a load of frustration before exiting in the form of verbal abuse, which continues to this day. She frequently reminds him that he is a failed artist and if she weren't associated with his dismal reputation she would be awash in artistic fame and adulation.

Their life has taken on the sameness of a movie rerun — she has tried other art forms but the outcome has been failure. Because of their need for money, Pablo regularly ventures into the streets to sell the small ceramic capons that she creates. His success has been limited and he has taken to panhandling. Every evening he presents Graciella the pittance he has garnered and tells her it is from the sale of her crafts. In order to maintain the fiction, he surreptitiously throws her capons into the lake. She berates him for the small amount of money and he apologizes, promising to do better next time.

Adriana sat for a long time without speaking. "It is a sad tale you spin, my perfidious painter. Graciella received no more than she deserved. Her behaviour makes sense only if there was something to be gained."

"I agree absolutely," I said.

I again beg your indulgence, dear reader. Our subterfuge has worked. So I say, thank you, a job well done. Congratulations to both of us.

I waved my empty glass at Adriana.

"You're like a sponge; you've sucked up the entire bottle," she said over her shoulder as she went to the kitchen to fetch another. "Tell me, old soak, what is your personal experience regarding the three types of women?"

By now, I had drained away sufficient brandy to float my guard down to a level where I found myself, like a sinner in the confessional, disclosing some of my most closely guarded thoughts. "I confess that there have been times when I have let strong drink manage my existence. That experience has not been all negative. A major benefit of inoculating myself with alcohol is that it provides immunity from various maladies including the three types of women."

"Explain yourself, my vacuous vaccinator."

"The prospectors are not interested in me because, even if I acquire some money, it is converted to liquor long before they can stake a claim. Architects find it impossible to rebuild an unrepentant drunk — those that try find the foundation too sodden to sustain a new erection. Wardens too, are unsuccessful because their desire to control is weaker than my intransigent nature — I'm a stubborn sot who finds joy in ignoring all imperatives.

"So, you see, the only woman that might have an interest in me is one who has her own money, who is secure enough that she has no desire to redesign me, and who is satisfied with controlling her own destiny rather than mine."

I left Adriana on her patio and proceeded home. It occurred to me that she knows that I have no money, that she has not tried to change me though she frequently tosses insults in my direction, and that she makes only weak attempts to control my life . . . and so, were I in need of more than a partner in brandy consumption, she would qualify.

The walk, the story, and the brandy had all conspired to leave me tired and though it was not yet noon, I felt the need to rest. After all, dealing with prospectors, architects, and wardens in one morning can be exhausting and I believed that I deserved a short restorative.

Love Under the Boardwalk

SO WHAT, YOU MAY ASK, IS the outcome of this lifetime? What lessons have I drawn? Which experiences have been valuable in drawing those lessons?

Before I speak of my own travels on the bumpy highways that criss-cross the Kingdom of Love, it is necessary to shift into reverse and retrace some of the route. If we are to engage in discourse on the nature of romantic love then you, the reader, must know exactly what we are talking about. What is love and how do we define it? What are its components? What do we mean when we say we are in love? Is the experience the same for all?

Love has been concocted in many different ways but most would agree that the recipe calls for a mix of ingredients — tenderness, regard, deep affection, liking, caring, and devotion — all stirred into an emotional stew and served with a garnish of delight at the happiness and pleasure of the other. Adding side dishes of intense attraction and sexual desire results in romantic love.

Years ago I discussed the question of love with Adriana. She contributed a few pesos by adopting the role of cynic. Though she no longer spouts the gibberish she did when she was attempting to puncture my personal balloon, it may be useful to replay the conversation in order to illustrate the pitfalls inherent in one of the prevailing views of love.

I remember how adamant she was. "It's a sensation we get and it crops up purely by chance," she said. "It occurs when you meet the right individual and it's impossible to predict who that might be. When that person appears, love will happen, even to you, old man . . . as surely as extra brandy causes your features to improve and your words to disguise themselves as wisdom."

In accord with previous practice, I chose to ignore her insult. "You claim that we are helpless in the face of love, that we have no more influence on when it happens than we do on when the wet season will begin. Well, you're dead wrong, my scintillating sensation."

"Then enlighten me, oh proselytizing purveyor of pith."

"Very well, but you must listen. Love is not just a feeling that suddenly appears. It takes time. There are stages in its development — three of them — sometimes called A, B, and C for Aching, Bewitching, and Coupling. Aching is what causes one to initially leave the safety of isolation. It is akin to lust and the fuels that jump start it are testosterone and estrogen. The B or Bewitching stage is achieved when there is an attraction that causes you to focus on sex. This stage is fuelled by the chemicals that kick the brain into the pleasure mode and screw up other functions like your heart rate, your sleep, and your appetite. *Coupling* is the attachment or bonding stage where people learn to tolerate each other. It is sometimes wishfully called commitment."

Adriana slid forward on her chair. "You're twisting my ankle, old man. Love may indeed pass through three stages. Call them A, B, and C if you like, but they're not the ones you describe. The couple enters the first stage when they can't keep their hands off each other. The A could stand for sex Anywhere at Anytime. The B or Bland stage occurs later when sex becomes routine — when it occurs only in the bedroom and only at certain times. It is symbolized by expressions like, 'not now, dear, I have to weed the window box or your mother is on her way over'. The C or Cussing stage is reached much further along in the relationship. It could also be called the 'expletive' phase and it is characterized by the couple issuing copulatory imperatives to each other as they pass in the hallway." She leaned back grinning at her own wit.

"Well done, my lilting liver spot. Tell me, what's the acronym for The Woman Is Thick? You've missed the stage where one runs for cover when one-half of a duo prattles on."

Adriana had unwittingly stumbled upon one of the two most prevalent views of love — that it is a spontaneous sensation or feeling. The other thinking portrays love as a deliberate act of choice. The gulf between them is such that were each view held by opposite halves of a couple, the distance across their king-size mattress would become infinite.

When I mentioned this, Adriana stood and waved her finger at me. "You haven't let me finish what I was saying . . . and you also misunderstand. Although it's impossible to predict who your love-struck lumpkin will be, you are not a passive bystander when it comes to romance. There are steps you can take that will better the odds. You must obtain the qualities that the other person deems important. For men, there are two options: acquire power or acquire money. For women there is only one: become attractive or at the very least, generate some sex appeal.

Taking any of these steps makes one more desirable and vastly increases one's chance of finding love."

"That's extremely cynical, my sexy showpiece. Do you actually see the goal as getting someone to love you, to *be loved* rather than finding someone to love?"

"Yes, I do, and the goal is exactly the same for men as it is for women — to get a good deal. We want a bargain — someone who has all the necessary qualities but also exhibits bonus traits. It's not unlike purchasing a dozen eggs at the market and later finding thirteen in the bag."

"So finding love is like buying eggs. It's more likely that you'll discover a broken mess in the bag when you get home."

"No," she said. "I mean good qualities that come as a bonus — desirable ones — like when a rich or powerful man falls in love with a woman — it's a bonus for her if he is good looking or kind or has a sense of humour. Of course, he is a bigger bargain if she only has to give up a minimum of herself."

"That sounds like a solid foundation on which to build a relationship — give up your identity. Go ahead, tell it all. What's your prescription for men?"

"For men the best bargain is to get an attractive woman, ample sex, and as many other free goodies as possible — goodies such as an amicable nature (but not too amicable), intelligence (but not too intelligent), lively personality (but not too lively), plus the ability to cook, to be a good homemaker, and to be a superb hostess. All these are bonuses for a man, and he will proudly exhibit them, just as she will exhibit her over-sized engagement ring."

"Spoken like someone who has bounced, too many times, on the matrimonial mattress. You have to be rubbing my knee."

Adriana sniffed. "There's too much wool in your skull to penetrate. What is it about free trade that you find difficult?"

"If I were to summarize what you've said, it's that basically rich and powerful men offer goods and services for attractive women . . . and for their sexual favours. I can't think of another word but prostitution. You make every woman a whore. Implicit in your argument is that women are only interested in economics and not sex, that their libido is as flaccid as a naked man in an Arctic storm. If what you say is true, why have men wasted so much time trying to control women's bodies and hence their sexuality? They've tried everything: chastity belts, ridicule, mutilation, witch burning, mandatory face covering, insults, and medical goofiness. Everyone who has had even the most cursory relationship with a woman knows that it's all a lie. Except, perhaps, during Arctic storms, women visit Hornyville as often as men. They just drive slower cars to get there."

"Slower cars, my backside! Why should men set the standard? Maybe women are right on time. After all, our tanks are still full when men run out of gas." She poured herself another drink. "Go on, my frosty friend."

I held out my glass. "First, tell me how two people can come to love each other under your scheme, if one is looking for cheap goods and the other *is* cheap goods?"

"Again you misunderstand. Both are looking for bargains. They fall in love when each considers that he or she has found the best catch available considering their own intrinsic worth. Doesn't that make sense?"

"Only when trading a burro for a milk cow, my burdensome beast. Everything you've said is designed to cause failure. The fallout from your approach is disappointment and divorce. It's like buying a costly vehicle only to discover that there is no engine under the hood. Your phrase, 'falling in love', implies that one has no control as to if, when, and why one tumbles, and with whom one shares the descent. Every time it's uttered, a divorce lawyer somewhere moves to a more desirable neighbourhood and Hollywood cranks out another movie."

Adriana motioned me to silence. "Enough of this 'doomed to failure' rhetoric. Before you proceed, my licentious litigator, let me tell you about a young American couple whose acquaintance I made years ago right here in Aguas Profundas. They are an example of the happiness that surrounds people who plunge into love."

I retrieved a pillow and settled in to listen. Adriana's stories are often long and a chair can become very uncomfortable by the time she finishes. "Go on if you must," I said. "I'll try and stay awake."

She scowled in my direction and then told the following story.

Harold and Cecilia Wildebeest led lives that were the envy of everyone. In all aspects of the human body, spirit, and personality, each was a credit to his and her individual gender. Harold was tall and broad shouldered with dark wavy hair. His steady brown eyes exuded a quiet competence that signalled the ability to see the fundament in any situation. His smile was genuine and exhibited even white teeth below a nose that was neither too long nor too short and rested right where it should, in the middle of his rugged tanned face. Dimples appeared in his cheeks when he smiled, which was often for he had a sunny disposition that lit up every personal proceeding. He had a melodious voice and had once crooned "Under the Boardwalk" at his cousin Eigil's birthday party after consuming a number of Green Buddhas, drinks constructed mainly from crème de menthe. Females were prone to swoon when he entered a room and most of the time, the girdle he wore under his open-necked cowboy shirt was barely visible.

Cecilia inhabited a body that was a collage of schoolboy dreams. She was neither tall nor short with generous proportions in the right mathematical distribution so that she attracted the attention of every passing male. Long strawberry-blonde hair framed deep blue eyes that were capable of perforating any soul. Her beguiling countenance was enhanced by a quick smile that radiated good humour. It was also enhanced by glistening teeth, red lips, and a complexion that daily was enticed to glow by massive applications of makeup. It mattered little where she travelled her road and her face were always paved.

It was a foregone conclusion that, if both of them were not to be extraordinarily cheated, each would have to wed the other. And this they did. Perfect beings are rare outside of heaven and if not exactly a miracle, it was at least downwind from a miracle that they both experienced the phenomenon known as 'love at first sight' when they glanced into each others eyes at cousin Eigil's party. It happened while Eigil was entertaining his guests by flexing a large pair of pectorals which were clearly visible under a tight-fitting pink glitter shirt. Harold was singing "Under the Boardwalk" and Cecilia was distributing cocktails.

The effect of that glance was so powerful that Harold momentarily forgot the words to his song, and Cecilia dropped her tray, dousing the cigar that Eigil was smoking and splashing Green Buddhas across his pink shirt completely soaking his perfect pecs.

❧

Adriana paused to sigh. "They were a beautiful couple," she said. "Their marriage was flawless. They were always together and their love went on forever."

I could restrain myself no longer. "Stop right there," I said. "I too knew the Wildebeests. Yes, it started well but their marriage didn't last."

Adriana looked startled. "I lost track of them. They were so much in love. What happened?"

"Initially, the trouble seemed as minor as a passing cloud on a sunny day. It should have disappeared as quickly."

"Enlighten me. I can hardly believe they are no longer together."

❧

It was a long time ago. I had joined them for drinks after they had attended a concert by the Drifters with their friends Bill and Wilma Barnacle. Cecilia hadn't liked the concert very much. "They may as well have been drunk, the way they sang," she said.

Harold, who had been a fan forever and considered the Drifters just slightly above perfection, took immediate umbrage. "I understand why you feel that way," he said. "If musical taste was water, you'd be permanently dehydrated."

Everyone laughed including Cecilia. Then she turned away, formed her mouth into a hyphen, and sat in silence until Harold finally asked, "Just what group do you consider greater than the Drifters?"

Cecilia didn't hesitate. "The Chipmunks," she responded. "There's no contest." This time Harold didn't laugh. He sullenly sipped on his brandy and eventually muttered, "As I said, if musical taste was money, you'd be in the poorhouse."

I checked myself from pointing out that he hadn't said that at all.

An awkwardness settled over the table and I left early. When I saw them the following week, all appeared normal. However, as I soon discovered, life for them was anything but normal.

Cecilia spent the week brooding and thinking about other men — men with refined tastes, men who appreciated women with refined tastes, men who would never dream of taking her to a Drifters' concert.

Harold also spent the week brooding and thinking. He imagined a woman who understood good music, a woman who believed in the Drifters, a woman who knew all of the words to "Under the Boardwalk".

Though each was building a reservoir of resentment they attempted to normalize their lives by resuming activity in the bedroom. However, Cecilia's reservoir was filled to capacity and she could not refrain from criticizing — not large ugly criticisms, but small delicate ones, spoken quietly with just a hint of derision. "It's all right, dear," she said to Harold. "It'll be better next time."

"What do you mean, better?" Harold said. "No one's ever complained before."

"I've listened to the grapevine," Cecilia said. "Maybe they didn't complain . . . to your face."

Harold's ego had less strength than his jaw so it wasn't long until he moved out. I visited him in his basement apartment. He sat on a cot holding a beer, his cowboy shirt hanging open and his girdle on the floor beside an empty wine bottle. He seemed resigned. "I should have known from the beginning," he said, "when she spoiled my performance by spilling drinks."

Cecilia also confided in me when I ran into her during intermission at the symphony. "I should have known from the beginning," she said. 'He was only interested in his own voice. His cousin, Eigil was the one that paid attention to me. That's him over there." She pointed to a man standing by the bar smoking a cigar and wearing a pink glitter shirt.

She confessed that even in the thick of her love for Harold she had been unable to shake the image of Eigil's black chest hair quivering at the top of his open-necked shirt whenever he flexed his pectorals. She went on to tell me that she had a premonition of what might occur. Eigil frequently came to see Harold in the late afternoon after he got off work. Prior to each visit, without forward planning and starting early in the morning, she would exfoliate her face and body, shower, shave her legs and armpits, wax her bikini line, apply toe and nail polish, curl her eyelashes, put on foundation, powder, skin lotion, eye shadow, eye liner, mascara, deodorant, blush, perfume, and lipstick. She would also shampoo, dry, curl, mousse and spray her hair, pluck her eyebrows and upper lip, put on earrings, necklace, ankle bracelet, a new pair of panty hose and her most secret of Victoria's Secrets, as well as an alluring summer dress with matching pumps. Then, completely unaware of her own motivation and afroth with internal turmoil, she feigned indifference, all-the-while manoeuvring to preserve an unobstructed view of Eigil's shivering chest hair.

❧

Adriana interrupted. "So was that it? They never got back together?"

"No they didn't. I had thought of attempting the role of peacemaker but I knew it would fail. Their separation was permanent and there was no turning back. 'Love at first sight' is a euphemism for 'depleting resource'. There is no depth. The well is shallow and soon goes dry. Inevitably, new exploration becomes the order of the day."

"Are you saying that all spontaneous love is ill-fated — that falling in love is a prescription for a bad relationship?" Adriana asked.

"No, just that it's not the best model. If we think that love is a sensation then we do things to respond to that. We do that rather than behave in conjunction with our hopes, aspirations and values — behaviour which by its nature would provide a more solid foundation than feelings do for building a relationship."

"Okay, enlighten me."

"I'll do that another time, my impetuous imp. Right now, I'm tired." I said goodnight and left for home. On my way through Adriana's yard, I found myself humming "Under the Boardwalk".

Melting Schnauzer's Cataracts

Note to the reader: Neither i nor Adriana subscribed completely to the views of love presented here. However, I think it is a useful exercise to continue our time-warp and portray our conversations exactly as they took place those many years ago.

We were again on Adriana's patio and she was reinforcing her reputation for volume. "Let's hear it all," she said. "Pass me your speck of wisdom."

"I'll see what I can do. Before you brought up the Wildebeests, we were discussing 'love as a commodity'. The problem with that approach is that one never gets enough. It's not unlike striving for more money, or a gourmand looking for a better meal, or a competitive runner trying for a personal best. Women want more in a relationship . . . things like commitment, sensitivity, help with housework, togetherness, and attention. A man also wants more — perhaps for a woman to be wanton in the bedroom and an angel in public, or for her to become younger as he ages. Being loved is never sufficient."

"So, we want more. Why is that a problem?"

"It's a sword with two edges. Wanting more means that, relatively speaking, love is a non-renewable resource . . . and being finite, if it's based on such a flimsy foundation as 'love at first sight', it has nothing in reserve and is bound to deplete."

"Okay, suppose I believe you. What's the alternative?"

"The opposite view suggests that the consumption rate is such that love can be produced fast enough to maintain itself. Most would agree that this is the case with parental and brotherly love, but it's also useful to observe romantic love through the lens of sustainability."

"Tell me why."

"As I said, your observations are from the viewpoint of an individual wanting to be the beloved rather than the lover. He or she has high expectations and little incentive to become educated in the intricacies of romance, all of which results in arrested development. That train stops permanently at 'attraction' and rarely rumbles down the track to 'attachment', leaving the passengers befuddled as to where they are. The confusion exists because, during much of history, we humans have allowed religious and political institutions to define what romantic relationships should be. Nowadays, new-age charlatans and Hollywood also call the tune. Therefore, we twist ourselves into pretzels trying to fulfill roles that others have defined rather then chasing our own biology. To paraphrase a great philosopher, *You can choose what to do, but not what you want to do.*"

Adriana yawned, an unsuccessful attempt to appear bored. "Okay, if it's necessary, let's taste your pip of perception. Tell me what love is."

"Anytime, my misshapen misanthrope. The alternate view doesn't see love as a passive undertaking, where you sit on an inert rear-end and wait for romantic fireworks to spontaneously explode around your head. No, it's a choice where you look for someone to love, find him or her, and then commit yourself to that individual's happiness. As we each drive a different road to happiness, love and its twin sister intimacy must be learned anew with each fresh situation."

"What do you mean by learned? Do you want to establish a degree program?"

"In a sense, yes. My primary goal has always been to discover the nature of love so that we humans can better rectify the fallacies that surround all aspects of that subject. I now understand that love is actually a blend of science and art, and like any science or art, it must be approached and studied with the right attitude and from the right angle — from the point of view of finding someone to love — not of finding someone to love you. The distinction is subtle but important. The approach requires that we make the effort to acquire the keys to another's happiness. It's not unlike the resolve, focus, and endurance needed to learn music or art . . . or even engineering, and like those subjects there are three requisites: first we must learn the concepts, then we have to master the mechanics, and most important, we should want to do it. Attitude is everything — one's ability as a lover is primarily determined by *how* one dwells in one's own head."

She leaned forward. "The image of you living in your head makes me think of a jackass residing in a coffin . . . and speaking of mastering mechanics . . . the last time you adjusted my carburetor, you ended up spilling lubricant on my rear axle. You're lucky I didn't dismantle your drive shaft."

"No, I mean it. Love starts in one's own head, but not as the result of a fortuitous, emotional accident as you believe. It may be a strong feeling but it's also a judgement, a decision, and a promise."

"Aha, my ancient artefact, you're scalped with your own scissors. You haven't lived in that manner. As far as love is concerned you've danced across the map. You speak one way and move in another. That's hypocritical."

"Not so. Like any student, I did not start with full knowledge of my subject. I said that you have to commit to another's happiness. I didn't say for eternity. Nowhere on our romance genes is there a code for duration or exclusivity. If you like, I can give you an example of love as I have described it."

"Please do. So far you make sense in the same fashion that a rooster makes eggs."

🐍

My tale concerns Melissa, a young lady of my acquaintance, and her pursuit of Antonio, a gentleman she met at a party arranged by Antonio's older sister, an intimate friend with whom she had gone to college. She determined that here was a man that she would like to know better. Accordingly, she asked if he would like to meet her one day for a coffee. He said he would love to. The next day she phoned to arrange a time and place. He was busy. She tried again on the day following with the same result. In fact, she phoned every day for a week and he was otherwise occupied at each time she suggested.

My friend does not daunt easily. She found out that he lived in her neighbourhood and caught the 7:33 bus every morning to go to his job in a pet store where he was apprenticing as an assistant cage cleaner, a position that gave him the same standing with the owner as a tree has with a dog. On the Monday following the week of fruitless phoning, Melissa made her way to the bus stop at 7:33 AM. Antonio nodded to her and she followed him onto the bus. She sat next to him and asked him to have lunch with her that day. He replied that his job at the pet store was arduous and that he never went for lunch. She then asked if he would meet her for dinner. He turned her down. "Prior commitments," he explained.

With her efforts again fruitless, Melissa decided that she was searching in the wrong orchard. Accordingly, she expanded her horizons. She determined to find out what it was that gave Antonio satisfaction and made him happy. A discreet and ribald discussion with the sister led to the discovery that he had but three passions in life: he raised rare soprano canaries; he lobbied for the protection of the world's one remaining herd of wild Iranian goat-eating ocelots; and he occasionally locked himself alone in his closet where he engaged in wild imaginative sex assisted by pictures of Big Red Machine, the local women's soccer team.

After digesting this information, Melissa joined SCAT, the international organization of Soprano Canaries and Trainers, enlisted in conservation efforts to save Iranian ocelots, and began taking soccer lessons.

A few weeks later, she caught the 7:33 bus and again sat beside Antonio. During the ride she pontificated on the difficulty of training canaries and waxed eloquent on efforts to preserve foreign ocelots. Antonio was intrigued and they started to meet occasionally for coffee and conversation. One day, he mentioned that Big Red Machine was playing a home stand and that he had never been to a soccer game. Melissa bought tickets and they went together.

The ice hadn't completely melted but the temperature was up a few degrees. They began attending soccer games, but Melissa found their relationship frustrating. It always halted at the final whistle, although Antonio occasionally allowed her to escort him home after a game. One evening, after she had brought him home and he had rushed inside to lock himself in the closet, she sat down on his front step, pondered their future and conjured up a new strategy. The next day she purchased a small tent and pitched it on Antonio's veranda. She began sleeping in the tent, rousing each morning to escort him to the pet store.

Weeks passed and winter approached. One cold night, Antonio opened the door and invited Melissa to come in before she froze to death. "You can sleep on the floor in the kitchen," he said. She moved in and every night she surreptitiously moved her sleeping bag a few inches until it was positioned outside Antonio's bedroom door. One evening he carelessly left the door open. Melissa quietly moved her sleeping bag to the foot of his bed and placed it beside Schnauzer, Antonio's ancient pet dachshund. Schnauzer did not approve of this arrangement and pulled himself onto the bed where he hunkered down and slept across Antonio's feet. This situation persisted well into the dry season.

Melissa was close to exhausting her mental and physical resources and, in this state, she frequently neglected to eat. Soon, she was experiencing erratic blood sugar levels in spite of helping herself to the left-over pizza that Antonio set out for Schnauzer. One evening, slightly afuddle from constantly propping up blood sugar with second-hand pizza, she threw caution out the window and crawled onto the bed. Schnauzer snorted a protest, shook his head to evenly distribute a large amount of drool and moved back to the floor.

The new arrangement lasted until the end of the summer rain — Melissa dozing alone at the foot of the bed, weak and barely able to arouse herself in time to catch the 7:33 bus. One morning, still perched at the edge of her quest and within easy hailing distance of defeat, she had a flash of insight, so brilliant it melted the cataracts in Schnauzer's eyes. She accompanied Antonio to the pet store and then left to spend the afternoon shopping. That evening she donned a brand new Big Red

Machine t-shirt before crawling onto the foot of the bed. Antonio offered an extended grin, lifted the blanket, and invited her to join him. Schnauzer, whose hearing was acute, pushed open the door and moved into the tent on the veranda.

The breakthrough was complete. Melissa had mastered Antonio's happiness. Eventually, they bought more T-shirts, transformed the closet into a recording studio for canaries, and tied the wedding knot. Their feelings for each other are so profound, so intimate, and they communicate so fully that their marriage has lasted for more weeks than their courtship. They continue to attend soccer games, train canaries, and they have adopted Anoush, a homeless Iranian Ocelot who lives happily in the tent with Schnauzer.

Melissa and Antonio's love sounds like cotton candy, tastes like neon, and sparkles like an operatic aria. Likewise Schnauzer and Anoush exist in perfect harmony although the tent now smells like the plural of armpit. The prognosis is that both of these relationships will endure.

🐚

Adriana was roaring. "I've heard of love causing the earth to jump," she cackled, "but love that causes an ancient daschund to move must be very profound. Perhaps you've stumbled onto a new standard for unrestrained feral romance." She paused to wipe away tears and then abandoned herself to more hysterical mirth. "The wooing took longer than most people's life expectancy," she gasped. "Did they start a family . . . or did taking care of a dog, an ocelot and canaries fill all parental imperatives?"

"Laugh if you must, but the story illustrates precepts that were hidden in the baggage we humans carried across the starting line."

"What do you mean?"

"From the beginning, we have all wanted to 'be in love'. But being in love is not love. Love is the ore that remains after *being in love* is sluiced away . . . and that ore is not a limited commodity."

"I agree to the extent that forcing our biology to obey society's rules has proven as successful as telling a cat to heel. I also agree that love and intimacy should have more prominence in relationships."

"Certainly they should, and they do when institutional conditions such as marriage, divorce, and monogamy take on less importance — which is the case when the goal becomes the other's happiness rather than the other's fidelity."

'But you have to admit that marriage is popular."

"Of course it is. It works! Marriage and its first cousin monogamy are embraced by most religions and governments. Priests and politicians love them. They are effective antidotes to passion and hence contribute to order and civilization. Passionate love is dangerous and the ideal citizen should have no appetite for it."

Adriana was suddenly serious. "But will having happiness as the goal guarantee perpetual bliss?"

"Of course not. It can only tip the odds. We all know that some conjugal mergers are ill-matched and pitiful."

"Yes, they are . . . but why?" she asked. "For example, what is it that makes us so ill-matched? Is it because I have inherited a surplus of wisdom and God's inventory was low when you were born?"

"If love correlated with wisdom, my religious relic, your most romantic encounter would have been with your shower. Love is never an egalitarian experience. While both parties must participate, it is impossible for them to participate equally. Just as no two people exhibit identical patterns of baldness, no two experience the same pattern of love. Why is this so, you ask? Because, rarely are the tasks of lover and beloved approached with the same intensity by both parties.

"It doesn't matter from what angle you observe it, love is a perilous undertaking not to be tried by those in a weakened state. The chance of finding eternal happiness is minuscule. The probability of failure is almost as high as the probability that a priest will enjoy little success at celibacy.

"To achieve the other's happiness is not just to facilitate those things that give the other well-being, security, and contentment. There must be more. We must endeavour to help our partner become everything that is possible for him or her. We must also ensure that no element of coercion exists, so that each half of a relationship feels completely free to become the person he or she wants to be. This precludes all narrow concepts that serve to inhibit."

"What are you talking about? Give me an example."

"I'm talking about things like obedience and jealousy. Neither of them can exist without a sense of ownership and, when one person has that sense, then the relationship takes on many of the characteristics of slavery."

Adriana wanted to talk but I was tired and the night had inexplicably turned cool. I buttoned my sweater and made my way home. As I crawled into my cold and uninviting bed, it dawned on me that Adriana is right about my not treading the path I have so carefully defined. While I have always endeavoured to ensure my partner's happiness, I have not always left the door open so that she might ensure mine. It seems that there are two doors and one is as important as the other.

Flying Avocados

I HAVE SAVED THE BEST FOR LAST, although the tale is never ending. A number of years have sped by since I began this story on my eightieth birthday. I must tell you that on a more recent birthday Adriana invited me to have breakfast with her. She then suggested that if we were to eat together in the morning that I may as well spend the night. She also said that if past performance gave any indication of future accomplishment, I would probably be ready for breakfast soon after going to bed. She smiled and a strange look came across her face. "Perhaps you would prefer to stay for lunch and dinner as well," she said.

This sudden turn of events startled me and I came near to being at a loss for words. Fortunately that fate has not yet befallen me. Previously, when I invited Adriana to meander on my mattress, she had scowled and asked, "Have you considered your predicament if I say yes?"

"I'd love to stay," I said. "But what brings this change of heart?"

"There's no change. I believe that one is never too old to make a dim-witted decision. Besides, I've always maintained a tender spot for you and I thought it was time to raise the stakes on our relationship. Maybe we are like salmon swimming upstream. If we throw ourselves at a waterfall enough times we may get lucky and gain the next level. Otherwise we risk spending the rest of our days swimming alone in a pool we should have jumped over years ago. More to the point, it concerns me that I have a drawer full of sexy underwear that no one has seen."

As a man ages he frequently finds that he needs more care than that provided by his own resources. Whether it be nurse or live-in companion, he will inevitably be told when, what and how much to eat; when he should go to bed and to the bathroom; when to bathe and at what time he may visit friends; what shows he can watch and where he may travel; how much money he should spend and on what he should spend it. In other words, by simply assuming the cost of a caregiver's salary, he gets all the benefits of marriage . . . and wonder of wonders, here was Adriana offering me a similar situation without the out-of-pocket expense. How could I refuse?

"I have waited for this day," I said. "However, I'm grateful that neither of us is capable of spawning. I understand that the result of that endeavour is a quick demise."

That conversation was months ago. Since then I have only returned home for brief periods. Adriana's place is not large and yesterday we bumped heads in her kitchen when we both bent at the same time to retrieve a fallen spoon. "Damn," I said. "This is ridiculous. Your house is too small. Why don't you dispose of it and we can move into mine."

She didn't hesitate to reject my invitation. "No," she said. "There will be times when we will each need our own space."

"Why is that important? Surely it's better to be together."

"Not always," she said. "It's important because separation implies movement which is the antithesis of the status quo — it negates inertia. There are times when we will need to be away from each other if only to come together again. Movement generates touching and that produces intimacy. I know it sounds strange but being apart promotes closeness."

"I gather that's what you meant when you referred to the next level."

"Yes, it is. That's why we need to stay in my house. Smallness promotes intimacy. We need small: small rooms, couches for two, undersized beds, tiny tables, everything. To live here together forces us to touch. In a sense never intended, size really does matter." She chuckled. "It just occurred to me, my minute maestro, that given *your* size, we should be the most intimate couple on the planet."

I have to admit that Adriana is correct about one thing. Houses should never exhibit ridiculous size and conformity. I know that many men and women adore monstrous homes and they are promoted in every magazine on the newsstand. But the dead space in these gigantic mausoleums encourages us to lead stupefying lives and to have even more stupefying relationships. A house's main function is to create dreams, not a sense of loneliness. Of course, the bedroom should always be reserved for fantasy, and never for wishful thinking.

Adriana and I already exhibit the defining feature of all long-term couples — we finish each other's sentences — although anticipating what she is going to say is not always pleasant conjecture. Nonetheless, she maintains that familiarity is never repellent in the same sense that sweet is never sour. She also says that a lack of intimacy forces many lovers to become nothing more than copulating roommates.

"That's not all bad," I said. "The only thing worse than being in a loveless marriage is being in a sexless marriage. If it's true that an intimacy deficit leads to copulation then it might be desirable to fight more often."

She responded by throwing an avocado which found its mark just above my left cheek. I waited the entire afternoon for the predicted copulative experience while holding a cold cloth to my discoloured eye. I admit that I am not a mathematician but I swear that for the next week, I detected no increase in the frequency of our couplings, sexual or otherwise. Perhaps flying avocados do not qualify as a lack of intimacy.

"I'm sorry about your eye," she said. "I have no wish to hurt you, although I keep that option open."

'But I didn't do anything," I protested.

"Yes, you did. You twisted my sentence. The avocado was a warning — a demonstration of what could happen should you twist again."

As you can see, we are not always almonds and honey. That mixture is sweet but it can also be a sticky mess. We do not keep pets so when it is necessary to growl we must do it at each other. There are even times when I retreat to my house and howl at the chandelier in my dining room. Then, I ponder what life was like when I lived alone.

Howling and pondering usually provide enough incentive to my good sense so that it steps out from its hiding place and steers me back to Adriana's house. If enough time has passed, then her good sense has also reappeared and we retreat to our fantasy room until all the frost has melted from our attitudes. While I won't speak for Adriana, I am sure that she feels as I do — that we are both fortunate to no longer rely on walls for company.

We have accomplished all this behind a curtain of rudeness, sarcasm and ridicule. However when the curtain is raised, there on stage for all to see, is the first act of a drama which may be either tragedy or farce but which we both believe is also a love story. Please don't misunderstand. Adriana has not stopped her insults and I have not abandoned mine. They are like magnets that occasionally repel but more often they make us laugh, which causes our different polarities to come together. Laughter is extraordinary medicine and may well function as the best aphrodisiac for old people. It serves to blunt the sharp edges on all the foibles, ills, and nasty moods that we have accumulated during our long lives and which we tuck away in secret nooks so that they are handy when we feel our self-image is in danger of being neglected.

I believe that Adriana is the silver lining that surrounds my cloud. In her mellower moments she says the same of me, which, of course, serves to contrast our current state with previous imbroglios. The comparison helps to alter our behaviours as we both strive to separate from the past so that we may gain all possible enjoyment from our present situation.

Speaking of separating from the past: I began this treatise with an account of my imperfections, particularly my fondness for my favourite relative — Uncle Brandy. I would be remiss were I not to inform you, the reader, of the prevailing status of that association. As I have aged, the relationship has matured from that of a controlling uncle and incorrigible nephew to one that resembles bemused encounters with an eccentric cousin. Age and decreasing energy have served to mitigate volume and behaviour, and while I have no desire to sever ties completely, I have found a suitable compromise. Many afflictions that attack in old age are ignored. For example, some cancers progress so slowly that they are allowed to remain unmolested. Medical experts reason that the victim will die of old age before the cancer claims him. I have decided that my affinity for alcohol is the same. Hopefully, I will be attending that great cocktail lounge in the sky long before my predilection asserts itself to the degree that it hastens my departure from the bar down the street.

Recently, in a moment of candour, Adriana expanded on her decision to share her life and home. "It was only after I was certain that you were no longer under the control of your uncle that I made my invitation," she said. "My house is too small for the three of us."

The reader no doubt understands that more than a few gallons of water have flowed to the sea since I last attended an educational institution. However, I feel as though I am again a student. Daily, I pursue studies that I hope will allow me to matriculate in the School of Sporadic Bliss with a major in Adriana and a minor in Female Moods. Adriana claims she is attending the same institution although, being Adriana, she insists that her research is at a post-doctoral level. She also says that I am a near-perfect subject of inquiry, second only to a laboratory rat.

By this method we hope to prevent the wonder from transforming itself into the mundane. Nevertheless, our lives have taken on predictability. I am now an indentured apprentice studying Adriana's needs. She, occasionally exhibiting a dollop of sympathy, tilts those needs toward the reality of my capabilities, which she has come to understand because she also is serving an apprenticeship, although she hastens to explain that a woman is interested in only one of a man's needs — that is, his need for her.

As this wheel turns, the hot flashes generated by our relationship cast kaleidoscopic patterns of shifting expectations on both of our lives. Once, we searched in different pastures but what we both looked for could not be found, it had to be made. We each tend to an appreciation of the person the other is becoming and that brings me to my own secret — the reason that I am arguably the world's greatest lover is that Adriana is also a great lover.

Let me explain. A lover can be no more impressive than his or her beloved. It is only when the desires of the person you love converge with your abilities to meet those desires that the possibility of grand love exists, and when that situation occurs it is impossible for you not to become as great as your beloved thinks you are. Then, as the poet says:

In the love you ideate,
It's impossible to overrate,
Any lover you create;
Only you will be as great.

Acknowledgements

Producing a novel is such an extended journey that a writer incurs many debts along the way, debts that are impossible to repay but which must be acknowledged.

To the people who were instrumental at the start of my writing journey, especially Graham Chandler and Patrick Carmichael. Thank you.

I would also like to acknowledge the contribution of Dolores, Greg, David, Barbara, Joei, Laura, Linda and Duncan of Pen and Inklings, and also of the Ajijic Writers Group which is too large to name individuals. Members of both groups are great friends and offered valuable criticism.

I'm grateful to everyone at Thistledown Press who have been so generous and supportive, and who smoothed away every wrinkle in the publishing process. I'd especially like to thank Kimmy Beach for her insight and guidance. No one ever had a better or more congenial editor.

Loads of gratitude to my family, especially Judy, my wife of fifty years, who willingly read every word, who has a quirky sense of humour and who, because she thinks nothing I write is funny, sets the bar very high. Every writer should be blessed with such a friend, critic, and love.

I have gained inspiration, ideas, and knowledge from a large number of sources, and although there is not room to mention them all, I'd like to list those that were most important. Gabriel Garcia Márquez's novella *Memories of My Melancholy Whores* and Jeremy Leven's movie *Don Juan DeMarco* provided the spark. J.P. Donleavy's *The Ginger Man* taught me that humour must have an edge. Dorothy Parker's short stories and L. Rust Hills' essays showed me how that edge could be applied. Dave Barry's *Guide to Marriage and/or Sex* and Steve Martin's *Pure Drivel* prove that silliness is always in vogue. All have had influence on this book.

Portions of the novel have been published previously. Excerpts, in slightly different form, first appeared in *El Ojo del Lago* (Mexico).

Neil McKinnon was raised in Saskatchewan and served in the Royal Canadian Navy before working as a businessman, archaeologist, university lecturer, and freelance writer in China, Japan, Mexico, Canada, and the United States. His articles have appeared in Canadian, Japanese, Mexican, and US publications, and his book *Tuckahoe Slidebottle* (Thistledown Press, 2006) was shortlisted for the Stephen Leacock Award for humour and the Alberta Literary Award for short fiction. He has served on literary juries and has edited and published academically. When not visiting family in Vancouver, McKinnon lives in Mexico.